"Eric Dinerstein, a world-class scientist who knows the ecology of the Himalayan region better than almost anyone else, has turned his razor sharp intellect to fiction in his enchanting debut novel, *What Elephants Know*. His deep knowledge of wild animals, lush landscapes and the rich culture of Nepal permeates through this poignant coming-of-age novel. It's as much fun as bouncing on an elephant back through the swampy tall grass, looking out for the hidden tiger!"

—K. Ullas Karanth, Director for Science-Asia,
Wildlife Conservation Society

"Now and then a book comes along that no electronic device can compete with, a book that encourages people to go outside and create their own adventures. *What Elephants Know* is a powerful story full of wonder. Readers won't want to put this book down as they experience Nandu's deep connection to the jungle and all its inhabitants."

—Richard Louv, author of *The Nature Principle* and *Last Child in the Woods*

"Elephants, it is said, never forget, but it is certain that if you read this book you will never forget it. Dinerstein takes you on a journey which extends through knowledge and adventure into wisdom."

—David W. Macdonald, CBE, Founding Director
of WildCRU, Oxford University

"No creature better embodies the delicate, paradoxical relations between humans and the rest of the natural world than the Asian elephant, wild but tamed, faithfully servile but majestic and proud. Eric Dinerstein's book movingly explores that relationship as it plays out in the life of one young boy, Nandu, a proxy for us all."

—David Quammen, author of *The Song of the Dodo* and *Spillover*

"*What Elephants Know* is an engrossing and evocative tale. The pages shine with deep understanding of local cultures and the natural world. It is an entrancing journey of the heart, rich in imagination and suffused with compassion for all creatures. Readers of any age will treasure this novel."

—George B. Schaller, Panthera and Wildlife Conservation Society

WHAT ELEPHANTS KNOW

ERIC DINERSTEIN

Disney • HYPERION

LOS ANGELES   NEW YORK

Copyright © 2016 by Eric Dinerstein

All rights reserved. Published by Disney • Hyperion, an imprint of Disney Book Group. No part of this book may be reproduced or transmitted in any form or by any means, electronic or mechanical, including photocopying, recording, or by any information storage and retrieval system, without written permission from the publisher. For information address Disney • Hyperion, 125 West End Avenue, New York, New York 10023.

First Hardcover Edition, May 2016
First Paperback Edition, May 2017
10 9 8 7 6 5 4 3 2 1
FAC-025438-17090
Printed in the United States of America

This book is set in 12.75-pt Spectrum MT Pro/Monotype; Qiber/Fontspring
Designed by Maria Elias

Library of Congress Control Number for Hardcover: 20115024177
ISBN 978-1-4847-4647-9

Visit www.DisneyBooks.com

To elephant lovers everywhere

Sooner or later we have to see that what we do and what happens to us are the same thing.
—Zen teaching

PART 1

DEFYING THE KING

Important italicized words are defined at the end of the novel. See page 271.

ONE

My mother is an elephant and my father is an old man with one arm. Strange, I know, but true.

For a short time, I was under the care of *dhole*,* wild dogs that live in the jungle. Before the *dhole*, I had a different mother and father who tied a red string around my neck and left me alone in the world. They believed the red string would give me protection. I do not know what became of them or why they abandoned me.

My father is the head of an elephant stable in the southernmost part of Nepal. He is called *Subba-sahib*, a title of great respect that everyone uses, including me. The older drivers also call him Old One Arm, but never to his face. I also call him Father, but only inside my head.

For fifty years, our elephant stable has been maintained by order of the King of Nepal—all so that once a year the king and his family can ride into the jungle on our elephants to hunt tigers. The stable exists in the Borderlands, a region far from Kathmandu, the capital city.

Our camp is at the edge of the forest, where tall trees and dense vines push right up to our stable. Our jungle is wild, beautiful, and dangerous, filled with rhinos, tigers, leopards, crocodiles, snakes, and every kind of bird.

I have learned to be wary of wild animals, but never afraid.

On the day of my first royal hunt, my life changed once again.

The October air was damp at dawn; it reminded me of the monsoon that had just ended. There would be no more downpours, no more mud between my bare toes, only blue skies and warm afternoons before winter set in. His Majesty the King was due to arrive at the stable in two hours. The king's astrologers could not have picked a finer day to be out in the jungle.

My father took me aside by the morning campfire. "Nandu, you have learned much about elephants," he said. "You are ready to join the royal hunt."

I nodded, watching the low orange flames bend on the short fits of air stirring about.

"This hunt is our most important duty, Nandu," my father said. "If the king and his brothers and uncles do not kill a tiger this year, they may never hunt in the Borderlands again. So let us make the king and his family proud of us today."

I looked into my father's face, hard with worry even in the soft glow of the fire. I wanted to ask him if there was any other way the king might enjoy the jungle rather than to hunt a tiger. To shoot such an animal for sport seemed cruel to me.

"What do you say, Nandu?" my father asked, pulling me from my thoughts.

"We will make them proud, *Subba-sahib*," I replied.

My father let his good arm rest on my shoulder and whispered to me so that none of the other drivers could hear. "During the hunt, you must be absolutely silent, Nandu. Remain in the back, and stay on your elephant. Do nothing but watch. You are the youngest stable hand ever to join a royal hunt. Remember your place."

He paused before continuing, "And when the king raises his rifle, shut your eyes."

I told myself the hunt was worth it, that if it was successful, the king might give more money to the stable. Every rupee we had went to the care of our twenty-five elephants. We often did not have enough to eat, and not one of our drivers owned a pair of shoes.

I finished my tea and ran to meet Ramji in the elephant tethering area. The sun had come up, but a chill hung in the air. I was panting when I arrived, my breath drifting like smoke.

Ramji is the lead elephant driver on my team. He was assigned to Devi Kali when he was young, nearly forty years ago. Now he is old and bald and short, with a serious look on his face almost always. He is quiet, too. When Ramji breaks into a rare laugh, he looks like a different person.

This morning I was taking the place of his *pachuwa*, the number two driver, who usually stands behind the saddle and acts as a spotter. The *pachuwa* was sick and *Subba-sahib* did not want him sneezing on the royal family, or worse, scaring off a tiger. I was not really a *pachuwa* or even a *mahout*, the number three driver, who was assigned to help the camp cook feed the visiting drivers.

I was a stable hand who swept up elephant dung and fetched firewood. Even my hand ax was only eight inches long—not a sharp one like a real driver carries.

Ramji did not give me any orders—he was quieter than usual, nervous, too—so I set to helping him saddle our elephant, Devi Kali. My mother.

I should explain. In nearly every way a mother cares for a child, Devi Kali is that to me. And in every way a child loves his mother, I am that to her. She is also very smart and usually figures out how to solve a problem before her driver, or anyone else for that matter, even realizes there is a problem.

As soon as we were finished, Ramji and I led Devi Kali from the tethering area to her position in the hunting party with the other elephants. Nearby, I could hear the crowing of the jungle fowl and the wailing of peacocks. I had to breathe deeply; I was shaking, from nerves or the temperature, I could not tell.

Soon, a hundred elephants would be lined up to take part in the king's hunt—the twenty-five from our stable and the rest from the other royal stable in Chitwan. Those elephants had walked one hundred and fifty miles to be here for the king's hunt, and today my father the *Subba-sahib* was in charge of all of them.

Finally, it was time to load up the royal passengers. *Subba-sahib* stood at the front of the line with His Majesty, the King of Nepal; members of his family; and several ministers. They had all replaced the black suits they wore at their arrival with green jackets and pants to blend into the jungle.

We had never had so many royals at our little stable at one time. They almost outnumbered the drivers at our barracks. There are seventy-five men to look after our elephants. Each elephant has a team of three men—a *phanit*, a *pachuwa*, and a *mahout*. For the royal hunt, the drivers wore uniforms, the only ones they had, used just for this special day.

Walking toward us, my father announced, "Ramji and Nandu, you will have the honor of carrying the forest conservator-*sahib* from Nepalganj."

I was not expecting to carry someone of such high rank on our elephant, and even though Ramji didn't look at me, I could feel he was thinking the same thing.

It turned out the forest conservator-*sahib* was not expecting to ride with us, either. He was known as a *"thulo manche,"* a big man, not because of his large belly—which was easily the size of a watermelon—but because of his high position as minister of His Majesty's Forest Department, in charge of all the forests of western Nepal.

"Subba-sahib, why do you put me on such a slow elephant?" he asked. "She is so old she might die during the hunt. Give me a younger one. I should be carried on a tusker."

"Devi Kali knows what to do, Conservator-*sahib*," my father replied. "She has lived long and taken part in many royal hunts. She is brave and unafraid of tigers. You will appreciate her courage."

"And who is this child who stands up behind the saddle? There is no place for a boy on my elephant."

My face became hot. I wanted tell this Watermelon Belly that I had been riding elephants since I was six, but I knew the one thing I must do at all times today: keep silent. One of the king's party called for my father to return to the front of the line, so he had no choice but to turn away, leaving Watermelon Belly's words hanging in the air.

Ramji spoke for me and for Devi Kali. "Conservator-*sahib*, do not be fooled by his young age. Nandu is eleven years old but already more skilled than many of the drivers you see here today. And we have only two tuskers at our stable. His Majesty is riding one and the prince the other. Both males are old, though, too old to even breed our females. You will see, they move not much faster than Devi Kali."

Watermelon Belly did not respond, as if speaking to a driver was beneath him. I wished I could tell him that he was not worthy to ride Devi Kali, who was wiser, stronger, and more courageous than most men.

TWO

The sight of one hundred elephants gathered together, trumpeting, rumbling, and snorting to each other, filled everyone with excitement. To ride elephants and hunt tigers with the king—for many, today would be the most adventurous day of their lives.

At last, the trail of elephants began to move. We crossed the Belgadi River by the stable and headed off into the jungle. It would be a half-hour's march west toward the Great Sand Bar River to reach the western edge of the Borderlands.

The familiar swaying movement of my body riding Devi Kali and the sound of branches breaking under her feet calmed my nerves. When you ride an elephant, you are a king, no matter your rank in the world.

I was deep in thought when a monkey screeched above us, making Watermelon Belly jump. I looked up into the tall fig tree, trying to keep from making a sound. A trio of monkeys sat together, eating figs, watching us march under their world.

We soon left the forest and entered the grasslands, where the thicket was so tall it swallowed up our elephants. I stood on the saddle to see over the tips of the towering grass, holding on to the towrope to keep my balance. The heavy morning dew flew onto us, like a gentle rain, as we brushed past.

We entered a large open area in the jungle, and I leaned over to look for tiger tracks in the sand. The sun had climbed higher in the sky, and its warmth felt good on my wet shoulders.

We were ten elephants behind the king, who rode on *Subba-sahib*'s lead elephant, the great tusker named Bhim Prashad. Every time the elephant turned his head, his huge ivory tusks glowed like crescent moons in the morning sun. I looked back to see the long ribbon of elephants following. It struck me then how lucky I was to be the only eleven-year-old boy in Nepal, perhaps the only eleven-year-old boy ever, to ride in the hunting party of the king.

When we reached the river's main channel, we crossed over to the islands, where the tall, thin rosewood trees stood staring at us. My father turned to me. His look told me that he had picked up a sign. I stood on Devi Kali again and saw the fresh track of a tiger in the sand along the beach. I could clearly make out its great footprints; if you rested a man's hat on one, the print would barely be covered.

Subba-sahib nodded to us and pointed to where he thought the tiger was hiding. He steered Bhim Prashad to position His Majesty for his shot and signaled Ramji to move Devi Kali just behind them. I saw Watermelon Belly smile for the first time that morning, pleased to be stationed so close to the king.

We were near enough that I could hear my father whisper, "The tiger's tracks lead into that patch of grass. We will wait here. When I give the signal, my team will drive the tiger out. You will need to take your shot quickly, Your Majesty."

King Birendra nodded. My father waved his arm, and seventy elephants with their riders quietly fanned out to encircle the tiger's hiding place. Watermelon Belly licked his lips and kept his eyes on the clearing, as if he were the one readying to take his shot.

Subba-sahib handed the king his rifle. I silently prayed to the jungle gods that His Majesty would miss.

My father whistled, signaling for the elephants and drivers to start shouting and banging sticks to drive the tiger from its hiding spot. The tops of the tall grasses swayed back and forth— from the breeze or the moving elephants or the moving tiger, we could not tell. The grass hid even the heads of the spotters standing on the backs of their elephants.

A sudden roar sent two of the younger elephants squealing in panic into the forest, their drivers and riders bouncing help-lessly on their backs. I wanted to tell old Watermelon Belly that he was lucky to be on my Devi Kali, who never flinched. But I kept silent.

Suddenly, a tiger of at least three-hundred pounds leaped into the open area and stopped. The king hesitated and then raised his rifle. The animal turned, and right away I recognized the one we called Chuchi.

Instead of shutting my eyes, as my father had told me, I leaped up and hurled my small hand ax straight at the tigress and shouted at the top of my voice. "Run, Chuchi, run!"

In a flash, Chuchi bounded gracefully away just as the king pulled the trigger. The bullet hit the ground where she had been standing. The words I had yelled echoed inside my head, but I could not hide the smile on my face. She was safe.

"You idiot! You spoiled the king's shot!" The forest conservator-*sahib* turned around in the saddle, his face red. I was afraid he would choke me. I knew I should sit down, but I could not move.

The king sat still and said nothing while his people murmured around him. The drivers and their royal passengers all looked at me and then at the place where the tigress had stood.

"Nandu, come here!" *Subba-sahib* called. "What did I tell you?"

The king held up his hand for silence.

I slid down from Devi Kali, walked to the king's elephant, and bowed low before him. My eyes rested on my dirty, bare feet.

The king spoke in a quiet voice. "Who gave you permission to scare away my tiger?"

"Your Majesty, I ask you to show mercy. Not on me, but on the tiger." My voice was steady, and I no longer felt afraid. I continued to stare at the ground. No one of my rank may ever look the king in the eye.

"Please forgive me, Your Majesty, but you were about to shoot a tigress, a mother to three young cubs. They would starve to death without her."

"How did you know it was a tigress with cubs?"

"Your Majesty, her name is Chuchi and I recognize her from the double-stripe across her shoulders. I have been to this spot with the *mahouts* to cut grass for the elephants. This is her territory."

"Your Majesty, the child is a storyteller," Watermelon Belly cried.

"Your Majesty," my father cut in, pointing to the trail between the tall grasses. Walking swiftly away from us was Chuchi, followed by three cubs close on her heels.

There was a long silence before the king spoke again. I did not care what he would say. He could put me in prison if he wanted to. Chuchi and her cubs were safe.

"Young man, it is the right and privilege of the Shah kings to shoot adult male tigers. But one must never shoot a mother tigress. You prevented a crime against nature. That is how I view it."

I continued to stare at my feet, hoping my relief did not show.

"Come, gentlemen," the king said. "We have had enough action for one day. Let us return to Thakurdwara. *Subba-sahib,* your son did right and deserves to drive his own elephant, or at least to carry a real hand ax." Everyone laughed at the king's joke, even Watermelon Belly, but his was an empty laugh.

I was relieved that Chuchi was safe, but when we returned to camp, I had a great shock. The king had forgiven me, but it was clear the elephant drivers had not. The older drivers would not look at me. It was as if I no longer existed. Every year there were rumors that the king could no longer keep two large elephant stables. One would have to close, and it would surely be the one where he had failed to get his kill. The drivers could not survive without the stable.

When we left that morning, I had felt like I truly belonged among the *mahouts*. Now I was the outsider again. As I had always been. If I were not the *Subba-sahib*'s adopted son, they would have sent me away.

I tried to loosen the ropes of Devi Kali's saddle, but my hands fumbled with the knots. Snorts of air burst through Devi Kali's trunk, which she twisted back toward me. I pressed my cheek against her rough wrinkled skin. I am sure she sniffed my tears. She rumbled softly, ruffling the top of my hair with her short breaths. To make myself feel better, I thought of Chuchi and her cubs being safe in the jungle. I had saved them, like my father, years ago, had saved me.

THREE

lephants know things about the jungle that not even *Subba-sahib* knows. I would never say so, but what we know is like a few drops of tea in the bottom of a cup in comparison.

A few days after the royal hunt, after the king and his men had left, I was riding on Devi Kali with my father. I treasured my time alone with him, away from the other drivers. Even more so now that most of the drivers had turned against me.

Just yesterday, I asked Ramji if he wanted me to take his turn cutting grass for Devi Kali, so he could keep his seat in the poker game he was playing with the *mahouts*. He barely looked at me and spit on the ground. The other drivers glared in my direction and said nothing. Without my friend Dilly, I would have no one to talk to among the drivers. At least I still had Devi Kali and my father.

Devi Kali's happy rumble checked my gloom. "*Subba-sahib,*

tell me the story of how Devi Kali found me and I came to live in the elephant stable." I liked to hear him tell it, in the way only he could.

"Nandu, I have told you that story at least a hundred times over."

"Yes, and I am ready to hear it again." I leaned back and looked at him from my perch on Devi Kali's neck.

"All right. I was out with Ramji and a couple of *mahouts*, teaching them where to gather *babiyo* grass. We had driven the elephants to Clear Lake to get a drink of water. Just before entering the lake, Devi Kali stopped and whacked her trunk against the ground. Then all four of the elephants brought their trunks down together, like a battle cry."

No matter how much time you spend around elephants, this sound always makes your heart race and your head prickle. The chances are good that something dangerous is nearby—a tiger, a sloth bear, or, worst of all, a king cobra rising from the ground, with its neck fanned and enough venom in its fangs to drop a tusker.

"The elephants knew something," my father continued. "Devi Kali raised her trunk over her head, sniffing the air. The others followed her lead. There was a sound of something moving toward us. Devi Kali stepped into the grass, gently pushing away the canes. There, sitting in a small clearing, was a little boy."

"Then what happened?" I asked. Devi Kali was holding her ears so still that I knew she was listening, too.

"I scrambled off my elephant and scooped you up, before you might be carried off by a leopard. It was a miracle you were still alive.

"Then the drivers made a wide arc to turn back to camp, looking for your parents. In a nearby area of grass, they found a large bare spot with the crisscrossing pawprints of a pack of wild dogs. *Dhole*, with their bright red coats and noses nearly as sharp as their teeth.

"Now, Nandu," my father said, resting his hand on my shoulder, "you know the *dhole* never sleep in the short grass; it is too open. These wild dogs had spent the night on guard, protecting you while you slept from all that could have easily killed you."

I nodded.

"You, Nandu, have a connection with the *dhole*. They are meant to look after you."

Devi Kali snorted.

"*Subba-sahib*, I think that the *dhole* are not the only animals looking out for me. I have Devi Kali, too." I reached down and hugged her neck. She rumbled back. "But keep going. The story is not over yet."

"All of us wondered why such a small child was left alone in the jungle. There was no trace of where you had come from, except for the necklace of red thread. It is worn by Buddhists, and this remains the only clue I have to this day about your first parents.

"The drivers thought you were a gift from the gods, maybe Ganesh, whose face took the form of an elephant. But they soon found out you were just a normal two-year-old, running all over the place and always underfoot," my father said.

The drivers were forced to put up with my antics, though, because soon after, *Subba-sahib* adopted me. What my father did not say was something I learned only years later: the only thing stranger than finding a child from north of the Himalayas abandoned in a lowland jungle, was for an old Tharu man to adopt a Tibetan child. Such lines were never crossed. My father never mentions this.

It was time for Devi Kali to bathe in the river. She bent one of her hind legs so my father and I could dismount. Then we watched her stride into the water, her trunk happily swinging from side to side, stopping for a moment to sniff the heavy air. Once she was chest-high, she dipped her trunk in the water, then lifted it in a great curl, spraying water on her forehead and back.

I swear, when she does this, I can see her smiling.

"Come, Nandu, let us sit on this fallen tree," my father said. I knew his gout must be bothering him again.

I leaned against my father as we sat watching Devi Kali. It was he who taught me that even though the elephants seem to serve us, we are truly the lesser beings. You see, my father is not only a *Subba-sahib*. He is from a family of *jhankri*—healers who can see into the future. He is a medicine man for humans and elephants and a *shaman*.

Subba-sahib can cast a spell or lift one.

When I was young, he taught me a prayer to honor an elephant. "Nandu," he said, "you must always first touch the elephant's skin, then touch your fingers to your forehead. It is a gesture of respect to a god humble enough to be our servant."

I have done this every day since.

In return, the elephants respected me, too. Quickly, I became known for having a special way with them. By the time I was six years old, I was appointed as a stable hand, whose job it is to sweep dung from the stable. A stable hand does not drive the elephants, but I soon became an exception. At age eight, *Subba-sahib* assigned me to learn how to drive Ramji's elephant, Devi Kali.

"Ramji, you must watch him closely," my father said. Ramji nodded and bowed. I was so happy, I jumped up and down, hugging first my father, then Ramji. When I went to hug Devi Kali, she wrapped her trunk around me and pressed me gently against her leg. I felt a comfort that I had never felt before, at least not that I could remember, not even with my father.

I felt, for a moment, that I was at home.

When Devi Kali was finished bathing, she climbed back up into the grass to graze and dry off in the late-afternoon sun. Finally, my father rose. It was time to head back.

"Let us stop in the village, Nandu."

"Yes, *Subba-sahib*. Perhaps we can get some sweets."

"Ha, we will see," he said, which is my father's way of saying yes.

Thakurdwara is a mile from our camp and like all Tharu villages in the Borderlands, is a cluster of houses made of wooden logs and elephant grass coated with mud.

We got down from Devi Kali, and I followed my father to the tea stall. He paid for a package of nuts and a paper wrapped full of strong-smelling cloves. He opened them and popped some in his mouth.

"Try some, Nandu. Cloves are good for the digestion."

I put two in my mouth and tried not to show how horrible they tasted. When he was not looking, I spit them out. I followed him back to Devi Kali, his bow-legged gait slower than usual. I hoped his gout would not worsen. Sometimes he must stay in bed for a week, and when he is ill I worry that I will lose him.

My father is not young. By the time he found me in the jungle, he was already over forty, which is old for a Tharu. Now, he is over fifty. But like many of his people, and like me, an orphan, he is not sure of his exact birth date.

He was married once to a young village girl from east of Thakurdwara. Six months into pregnancy his young wife passed away. After her death, my father devoted his life to running the stable. He never married again, and until I came along twenty years later, he lived alone in his tiny brick bungalow.

We rode back to the stable in silence. I watched the yellow ball of sun move lower toward the horizon, the long rays slanting across Devi Kali's head. I loved seeing the world from there, feeling the rough skin of her ears as she flapped them against my legs.

I think what I feel when I am with Devi Kali is what other children sense when their mothers hug them. When Devi Kali looks at me, I see love in her eyes.

FOUR

In the riverbank forest along the Belgadi the climbing rattan palm spreads out its fronds like fingers reaching for the figs in the trees above.

"Look, Nandu," my father whispered. A great hornbill flew into the trees. The giant bill, like a big yellow helmet worn backward, seemed to glow in the light. Two more landed in the figs, their black-and-white wings beating loudly. In the soft dirt track below, my father and I were searching for paw prints.

"Nandu, people in Kathmandu and Nepalganj read the morning paper to find out the day's events. Here in the jungle, we read tracks in the mud and sand to get the news important to us." *Subba-sahib* may have had trouble reading the printed page, but he was a master at piecing together the stories the tracks offered.

I walked ahead of my father, wanting to show him how much I had already learned. "Here, this looks like a young male tiger, leaving the area where he was born," I said proudly, pointing to an impression in the soil.

"Close, Nandu, but the track is a bit too small. Do you see clearly the round pad and four rounded toes? That is from a large male leopard."

I nodded, disappointed in my mistake.

"Now look again. See the grains around the toe marks and these narrow paired hooves? I would say a few days ago, our leopard walked here, maybe stalking a barking deer. My guess is the barking deer was waiting for the hornbills to drop down some ripe figs. The leopard was waiting, too."

We moved up a few feet. "Ah, look. Now we can compare. Do you see on top of the leopard tracks these footprints? They are from a wild dog. The *dhole* always leaves behind claw marks, but the leopard leaves none. The cats can retract their claws; that is how you separate their footprints from wild dog or jackals."

We were still stooped over the prints when the peacocks began wailing around the bend—*Meyaw! Meyaw! Meyaw!* My father motioned for me to get down and crawl to a hiding spot. Up ahead was something I had never seen before—two male peafowl dancing on the dirt tracks, their four-foot-long plumes spread into giant, shimmering blue-green fans.

They lifted and spread out their plumes with the big eyespots at the ends, trying to impress the females. Then they shook all over, making every feather vibrate and glint in the sun. "This is their ritual, Nandu," whispered my father. "They will dance like this in a trance until dusk."

Suddenly, before I even knew what was happening, a yellow-and-black spotted cat pounced on one of the dancing males. The others scattered up in the air, as the leopard slipped away, dinner in his jaws. I grabbed on to my father. I had no idea a leopard could be so close. They usually avoid us.

My father rose quickly and pulled me in the opposite direction, gripping my arm hard. He was still gripping it, in fact, even when we were safely outside the jungle. When he realized this, he dropped my arm, and we looked at each other, took a deep breath, and laughed in relief.

We cut through another village, Gobrela, which means "dung beetle" in Tharu. The villagers worked as hard as dung beetles, the men pitching hay and the women grinding grain in the courtyards. The Tharus grow wheat, lentils, mustard, and rice—lots of rice—and also graze their livestock in the jungle.

The villagers shouted greetings to my father and me as we passed, *"Ram, Ram, Subba-sahib."* They are proud that someone from their own caste is head of the king's elephant stable. Even the *Budghar*, the headman of the village, looks up to my father. There are few such positions open to Tharus, who are mostly illiterate farmers. Their children stay home, to help with the crops and livestock, even those of the *Budghar*, who is rich and has many kids.

Twenty minutes later my father and I were back in front of the campfire at the stable, holding mugs of steaming tea. My mind was still fixed on the dancing peacock that had been killed in an instant and then dragged away to be eaten.

"Why was the peacock not more careful?" I asked. "Did he know the leopard was watching him?"

"Nandu, sometimes in our lives we are like that peacock," my father said. "We must commit ourselves to do what is most important to us, without worrying about our fate."

FIVE

"Come on, Nandu, help me lift these bundles for Man Kali," called Dilly. I swung the grass heaps up to my friend, who was standing on top of his elephant.

Dil Bahadur, or Dilly, as everyone calls him, is my closest friend at the stable. Even though he is seven years older than me, we spend a lot of time together. Dilly's father, Bir Bahadur, was one of our best elephant drivers. I never met Dilly's father, though. He died more than ten years ago.

Bir Bahadur had been like a brother to my father, even though he was a Tamang from the hills and my father was a Tharu from the Borderlands. As soon as Dilly turned seventeen, my father assigned him as a *mahout* for the elephant Man Kali. Dilly was happy to take his father's place, which meant that he could move out of the one-room hut just beyond camp he shared with his mother and sister and into the drivers' barracks.

When I was old enough, we roomed together in the barracks

and stayed up late telling each other stories. His mother, Tulsi, still cooked for him, and for my father and me, too, out of gratitude.

Most of the other drivers have families, but they live far away. They are only together for the two most important festivals of the year, *Dashain* and *Tihar*. The rest of the time, the drivers live in assigned rooms and eat in the canteen.

Dilly's mother did much more than cook for me. She is a very smart woman and taught me to read and write and do numbers. Her father was a young mountain Tamang who had been recruited by the British Army to serve in India. So when Tulsi was young she learned to read and write in a proper school.

Every morning after Dilly and I returned from grazing the elephants, she made me sit down with Rita for lessons. Because he was older and could already read well enough, Dilly was allowed to skip off and drink tea with the other *mahouts*.

Though Dilly and I were friends, I had no use for his sister, Rita. She was always trying to prove she could do things better than Dilly or me—or anyone.

The feeling was mutual. Rita was jealous of me for many reasons: my friendship with Dilly for one thing; my work in the stable, for another; and that I could ride Devi Kali, while she had to stay home.

It is impossible for a girl to be a *mahout*.

Nearly every weekday, Rita and I sat at the table in their hut, patiently watching as Tulsi went over to the top drawer of her bureau and carefully lifted out a first reader for English and an old schoolbook that she had used when she was young. The time she took, you would think the books were made of gold.

Rita and I were in constant competition to be the best at reading and writing and numbers. Tulsi would make two sheets of problems and time us for two minutes to see who could finish more of the page. I had to work hard to beat Rita, which did not happen often, but when I did, she would turn very angry. Rita is three years older than me, so when I did win, it only increased her dislike of me.

I confess: I liked to make Rita angry, and winning was just as important to me, too.

Tulsi tried to keep the peace between us. "Nandu and Rita, you *both* are so quick to learn your lessons. You could be anything you want to be. Maybe you could go to school—"

But Rita would interrupt, "I do not want to go to school. I only want to be a *mahout*. If I cannot be that, I won't be anything."

Tulsi would pause quietly, then start talking about other jobs and lives that people lead far from the Borderlands, like doctors and engineers. Tulsi was determined that our lives would be different, that we would move away from Thakurdwara. I had no such plans for myself, ever. But there was no way to explain to Tulsi that my family was part human, part animal and that there were really no places where I could move and bring my elephant mother. So I just played along.

Rita is as tall as I am, very tall for a girl. When we race to the road, our bare feet kick up the powdery dust, and her long black hair flies behind her. I run faster, but she can climb a tree faster than Dilly or me or any *mahout* in the whole stable.

That morning, I had beaten Rita at both math and a foot race, and she could not hold back her tears. I felt bad, so I invited her to come with my father and me to go bird watching in the jungle. Like the sun had suddenly burst through a bank of clouds, she stopped crying.

My father was teaching me everything about birds he had learned many years ago from a British scientist named Dr. Jonathan Beardsley. The man had hired my father as his driver and guide, something that rarely happened in the Borderlands. *Subba-sahib* said it was the first time he had ever met a man who was not from Nepal or India. They had gotten along very well, and in just three weeks became good friends. As a parting gift, Dr. Beardsley gave my father his binoculars and his bird guide.

Now, my father knows every bird by its song or by the way it flaps its wings.

"Look, Nandu, Rita. That is the lesser flameback," my father said, pointing just over Devi Kali's head to an orange-and-black bird with a red crest. The bird flew across the grasslands, making big loops, as if looking for something it had dropped.

"His colors make him look like fire riding on the air," Rita said.

"Exactly, Rita," my father replied. "You understand where it gets its name."

I suddenly realized it was a mistake to invite her.

"What does the lesser flameback eat, *Subba-sahib*?" I asked.

"He is a woodpecker, so he drills into the tree bark and yanks out grubs."

"And what about that one? What is he doing?" Rita had spotted a bird with a black face, gray back, and white belly, carrying a green grasshopper.

"That is a shrike. A clever bird, Rita. He hunts his food— mice, grasshoppers, or maybe a frog—and then pins their bodies onto that prickly tree to eat later."

"Poor grasshopper," Rita said.

"If the shrike did not eat the grasshoppers, then the grasshoppers would eat all the grass, and there would be none left for the deer," my father said. "And the deer are food for the tiger. Life in the jungle is a giant spiderweb; if you touch one strand, it will vibrate at the other end. We cannot separate nature into good and bad, Rita. The gods do not will it so."

"Look, *Subba-sahib*, minivets." I pointed to a flock that had just entered a *kadam* tree, the males all red and black and singing loudly.

"Good eye, Nandu." He paused, suddenly. "Shhh! Do you hear that?"

"What is it, *Subba-sahib*?" asked Rita.

A flock of gray birds flew up from the ground, landed in a nearby tree, and began to chatter noisily.

"Rita, Nandu, pay attention. Here is a group of jungle

babblers. Their chittering warns us of danger nearby. There are always seven of them in a flock. Do not ask me why. Something must be headed our way."

A low growl from the bush announced the arrival of a large male tiger, who strode out boldly in front of our elephant. He glared at us and moved on, the silky black stripes in his orange fur rolling along his flanks.

"You see, if we remain silent and learn to listen, the animals tell us what we need to know."

Rita had never seen a tiger before.

"If we were on the ground, would the tiger have eaten us?" Rita asked.

"Yes," I said. "We would all be dead."

Rita leaned closer to my father, who patted her head. I definitely would not invite Rita out with us again.

"Don't worry. The elephants keep us perfectly safe."

My father gave Devi Kali the lightest tap with his finger, and she turned, heading back home, our three bodies rolling to my mother's gentle rhythm.

When we got back to Tulsi's hut, Rita and I turned into a pair of jungle babblers, telling Tulsi about the birds, their names, and what they looked like, while she cooked. My father interjected, too, mostly correcting us.

Dilly arrived just in time, singing for us the songs from the Hindi cinema. He serenaded Tulsi as she ladled spicy *dal*, mango pickles, and greens with chilis onto our plates of rice and chicken curry.

I had been regretting that I invited Rita to come with us, but then, sitting around in the hut, listening to Dilly sing and seeing Rita and Tulsi smile, I realized this is the closest I will ever get to having a true family.

I bit into a hot chili, and my eyes started to water. I looked at my father and he winked at me.

"Nandu loves my song so much it makes him cry!" Dilly said.

SIX

By early November, the air is chilled in the morning—perfect weather for *Tihar,* the biggest festival of the year. For five days, families gather to play cards and pray—not in that order, and not just to gods. There are prayers to crows one day, then cows, and finally to dogs—in honor of the creatures that live among us.

On the morning before the start of *Tihar,* I walked alone to Mohanpur, the village of my father's cousin, Garibuwa. The rice paddies that lay in long stretches on either side of the road had already been harvested, and a carpet of golden-mustard flowers had taken their place. The earth glowed bright yellow against the dark green-gray of the jungle beyond the fields.

Just before Mohanpur, I caught sight of a single red amaranth flower rising up in the middle of a field of mustard flowers. Taller than the rest, and a different color.

That flower is like me, here in the Borderlands.

I towered over the boys in Thakurdwara, all the villages really, yet I knew they looked down on me. My skin was different from theirs, copper-colored, like a mountain boy from the north. The kids who looked most like me were Dilly and Rita. They are Tamangs and have the same almond-shaped eyes and broad face as me. Tamangs are not common in the Borderlands. They are outsiders, too, but not as much as I am.

Whenever I was alone in the villages, I kept my eyes on the ground. I didn't want to meet the suspicious stares of the villagers. They treated me differently without my father or Devi Kali by my side.

By the time I arrived in Mohanpur, the dancers had assembled and a crowd had gathered. The men of the village were costumed in long, shiny feathers. They danced, shaking their plumes and shimmying just like peacocks.

I looked on with Garibuwa. When the dancers stopped for a moment, I told him about the time a month earlier when all-in-a-flash a leopard carried off a dancing peacock.

"Let us hope no leopard snatches one of our dancers today," he said, laughing.

The dancers spun around and around in a blur of feathers. I did not know how they could dance for so long without getting terribly dizzy. Two hours had gone by when the dancers finally finished. As Garibuwa and I turned to leave, I saw a cloud of dust rising in the distance. Surely it was my father, I thought.

It did not take long to realize that the cloud was approaching too quickly to be elephants, though. Soon I heard the sound of horses coming toward us, their hooves pounding the ground.

"Move! Get the children inside," Garibuwa shouted. "It's the Maroons!" Before I could do anything, Garibuwa had pulled me into his house.

"Nandu, stay here with your auntie until I am back."

As soon as he left, I grabbed a hoe and rushed outside. Through the dust I watched villagers running from men on horseback. There were seven riders, led by a man on a white stallion. They wore maroon bandanas to cover their faces. Everyone but the leader jumped to the ground and began ripping the gold and silver earrings, bracelets, and necklaces from the women and girls.

"Fight!" shouted Garibuwa. He swung his shovel and struck a Maroon in the ribs.

One of the dancers lunged at another bandit, yanking his bandana off his head. I stared at the bandit's face. He was a boy barely older than me. Our eyes met and my body froze. There was fear in his eyes.

The dancer could have easily killed the Maroon. Instead, he pushed him into the dirt and moved on. The boy pulled up his bandana and ran off toward the forest.

"Hurry!" yelled the one on the white horse as he lit a torch and flung it on the roof of a long house. The thatch roof crackled into a mass of smoke and flames.

I quickly dropped my hoe and joined the men throwing buckets of water on the neighboring houses. If they caught fire, too, the whole village would burn to the ground.

"Put down your axes, brothers, and give them what they want," yelled Garibuwa. Then he turned to the Maroon leader. "Kalomutu, take our money and gold but leave us our homes and our rice stores," he said.

Kalomutu waved to his men and tossed his burning torch into a low trough of water nearby. I listened to it sizzle. The rest of the villagers returned to their houses, quickly coming back with satchels and fabric bags stuffed with their life's savings.

After Kalomutu's men had collected the satchels and lashed them to their saddles, we waited for them to turn and leave. But they did not. One of the Maroons came riding up to Kalomutu with a newly lit torch.

The trumpeting of elephants suddenly filled the village.

Never had I seen Bhim Prashad move so quickly. My father was hanging on tightly. Ramji and Dilly rode on Devi Kali directly behind him. The air was filled with the sounds of elephants. The Maroons still on foot ran for their horses. My heart pounded in my ears as Devi Kali charged at Kalomutu, roaring.

Bhim Prashad followed. The horses spooked and reared up, nearly throwing their riders as they rode off, our elephants giving chase.

I watched as the Maroons disappeared across the mustard

fields, golden petals flying from the horses' hooves like sparks. Our elephants had saved the village, but they were too slow to keep up with the galloping horses.

"That was a miracle," Garibuwa said when my father returned. "Ten more minutes and they would have burned down our whole village."

My father spat. "When I saw the smoke, we set the elephants to run as fast as they could."

Devi Kali stood next to us, listening, her trunk circling in the air, trying to find any remaining scent of the horses.

"Will they return, *Subba-sahib*?" I asked. For the first time I realized I was trembling.

"They are far off by now, Nandu. I doubt they will return."

I watched the dancers pick up their trampled peacock costumes, anger swirling inside me.

"Garibuwa, was anyone hurt?" my father asked.

"Yes, several men were slashed. Some of the women have cuts, too."

"Nandu, Dilly, go shave some bark from the *simal* tree and gather some *ak* branches while you are at it."

For the rest of the afternoon, my father, Dilly, and I then went from house to house, treating the injured. Some of the knife wounds were quite deep, and the medicine my father made from the *simal* bark and *ak* branches burned. The villagers winced and a few cried out, but they were grateful for my father's skill as a medicine man.

Once we finished, we started on the trail back to the stable.

"Kalomutu feasts on the poor," my father said.

I was silent for some time. I could not help thinking about the attack, the sound of the horses' pounding hooves, the torch Kalomutu touched to the grass roof. And then I remembered the face of the young Maroon. A horrible thought popped into my head.

What if it had been the Maroons and Kalomutu who had found me instead of Devi Kali and my father?

"*Subba-sahib*," I said, "I saw the face of one of the Maroons. I thought he would look evil, but he looked like the village shepherd. He was barely older than me."

"Nandu, even baby-faced young men are capable of great cruelty."

Ramji spoke up. "I have never seen his face. But I have heard some villagers say that Kalomutu is from a wealthy family, not the son of an outlaw."

"If he is from a rich, high-caste family, why does he rob poor Tharu?" I asked.

"And why does he hide in the jungles and sleep on the ground?" Dilly asked.

"I will tell you why, Dil Bahadur," said my father. "No one bothers him in the Borderlands. There is no law out here. Kalomutu feels very powerful in this jungle district, more powerful than a *maharajah*."

We had almost arrived back at the stable. I stood up on our

elephant, eager to see our home, which had never been a more welcome sight. Surrounded by elephants and their drivers, the Maroons would never raid our stable.

I thought of the young Maroon again. I could not get him out of my head. Had fate not allowed Devi Kali to find me first, I could be in the forest with those men, counting coins and jewelry, instead of riding on her back.

I could have been a Maroon.

SEVEN

You can hear the Great Sand Bar River long before you see it. It roars like a wild animal during the monsoon floods. To Hindus, the water is sacred. They wade in to take blessing, though many cannot swim and risk being swept away. Even at low water, in November, the strong current races over the pebbles in the shallows, making a steady shushing sound.

My heart skips when I hear the voice of this wild river. It is the western edge of the Borderlands, my world, my home. I have no interest in what goes on beyond its banks.

Two weeks had passed since the attack by the Maroons, and normal life was finally coming back. Dilly and I had a free day, and so we took Devi Kali to go fishing. We dismounted, and I sent her off to graze along the riverbank. Across the channel a flock of cormorants worked together to herd fish into a shallow and all dove at once to snatch their meal. Suddenly, at the edge of the river I saw something moving. "Look, Dilly! It's a crocodile!"

A giant gharial male, armed with a trail of craggy scales down his back, crawled out of the water and lurched onto a sandbar. His thin snout and pointy teeth looked like an ancient sword.

"Nandu! I have never seen one so big. He must be twenty feet long," Dilly said. "He is a king."

"We bow to you, Crocodile King!" I said. We saluted him like he was royalty and laughed.

We found a spot to sit, a few hundred feet from the king. Gharial look dangerous, but their jaws are useless for biting humans. We baited our hooks with worms, dangled our fishing lines in the deep pool, and waited to see who would get the first tug on his line.

The day turned warm. The croc did not move. He was sunning himself, probably already full of fish.

"I dare you to swim across this river right now," Dilly said.

"No problem. He could not swallow me if he tried. If it were a mugger crocodile, I would send you first."

"That would be a match for me," Dilly said.

"The fish are not hungry," I said. "Let's cross over to the islands. I want to get rosewood for *Subba-sahib*."

I put the spools of the thick fishing line we use for catfish in the back pocket of the fishing vest Tulsi had sewed for me. We climbed on Devi Kali and headed out into the main channel.

The Great Sand Bar River flows fast and cold, straight down from the Himalayas to where it meets the Ganges River. I drove

Devi Kali into the current. The water covered her ankles, then her knees, and finally rose up to the bottom of her ears in the deepest part of the channel. The current was strong, so we held on tightly to her saddle. Although she was slow on land, Devi Kali was the best swimmer in our stable. Even if the water was over her head, she could easily make her way across a surging river.

We reached the shore of the largest rosewood island, the site of the royal hunt only five weeks ago. We would be sure to find downed wood here to carry back.

Unlike the tall jungle with its large trees and dense bushes, the thin young rosewood trees let the sunlight cut through them like long blades. Here it was brighter and easier to see birds. I wanted to search for them up in the canopy, but I kept an eye out for rhinos and tigers on the ground.

Suddenly, Devi Kali flapped her ears out wide. She had heard something and started moving toward a small grove of trees. We could not see anything, but then I heard a bleating sound from the dense grass.

"I know that call," Dilly said. "It is a rhino calf."

When Devi Kali crested the top of a small rise, a tiny rhino calf came galloping toward us. Devi Kali trumpeted a warning. The calf turned and quickly disappeared back into the wild sugar cane.

We dropped back down the rise. Up ahead was a narrow

ravine. When we entered it, we saw an old female rhino sunk deep into mud. She was not moving. I looked up in the trees where the vultures had gathered, waiting to start their feast.

"She got stuck in the quicksand," Dilly said.

"What should we do?" I asked.

"That calf will be killed by the next tiger that passes through," Dilly said. "There is nothing we can do, Nandu."

"We have to take her with us," I blurted out.

Dilly looked at me. He liked to take his time before making a decision. Me, sometimes I am like Rita, I cannot hold back.

"How will we get her to follow us? And what about the river? Do you think Devi Kali will simply offer her a ride?"

I did not want to say that Devi Kali would do anything I asked of her. That would seem like bragging.

"Wait, I have an idea," said Dilly. "The calf is probably hungry. Let's use the leaves off the rosewood branches. It's the rhino's favorite food."

"Yes!" I quickly began cutting branches.

"We will tie them into bundles, so we can distract her. Just watch, I know she will follow us," he said.

Soon we had a dozen small bundles, tied with vines, for each of us to use. I remembered the sound of a mother rhino. My father had taught me many calls of wild animals, but I never thought I would actually use one now.

"*Meeh! Meeh!*" I called to her.

Dilly and I listened. At first there was silence, but then the rhino calf began bleating back, slowly peeking out from the sugar cane.

Then in a flash, the calf came running. But when it was within ten feet of me, she stopped in her tracks. I tossed a few of the rosewood leaves toward her, and she rushed forward, sucking them up with her long upper lip. She was starving. We kept doing this for half an hour and the calf kept following us. Either the calf was starting to lose her fear of me, or she was too hungry to care who I was. I crouched down and soon she was plucking leaves right off the branches I held out to her.

"Grab the end of this, Nandu," Dilly said, throwing me the rope. He took the other end and looped it around Devi Kali's chest, tying a loose knot.

"Try to calm her down," he said. "Then we can put the rope around her."

We crawled to either side of the calf and stroked her ears and the top of her head. The calf began to breathe more slowly and to relax. She was no more than six months old, but she already weighed several hundred pounds. She looked funny—with her big head and short stubby legs—and not at all threatening. Even so, most elephants do not want any part of rhinos.

"Now what?" I asked. "Scratching her ears will not get her across the river."

"Let's loop the rope behind her chest and front legs. Then we will tie the other end to the saddle and tow her across the river."

"What if she goes under?"

"We will be there on either side to support her," Dilly said. "She should be able to swim just fine. The only problem I see is how will Devi Kali know how to cross without you on her back?"

"I will tell her."

"Nandu, there is no elephant command for 'tow a baby rhino behind you across the river.'"

"I talk to her all the time. She will understand."

I continued making the mama rhino's call, and the calf began to answer me while nuzzling my hand with her lip. As we walked up to tie the second rope to the saddle, the calf came along behind.

"I cannot believe it," Dilly said. "She is following us."

"Devi Kali, I know you do not like rhinos, but you must help us get her across the river. We will be right behind you," I said.

"*Agat!*" I commanded, and Devi Kali entered the river. "*Agat!*"

Devi Kali was already in the current and the rope was now taut, but the rhino calf would not budge. Again she began to bleat loudly. We rubbed her head like a calf does under its mother's chin and finally she followed us into the stream. The calf was a strong swimmer, but we made sure we stayed in Devi Kali's wake. She knew to angle up stream and break the current. Swimming together as a trio, the calf with Dilly and me on each side, we started to make our way through the great river.

Halfway across, I saw something break the surface—a pair of Gangetic dolphins. They were not a threat to us; in fact, they seemed to be offering help, steering us away from the deepest part of the channel. Maybe my elephant had called to them, her rumbling vibrating through the water. My father says many animals can speak to one another in a language we do not hear.

Twenty feet from the bank, the river became shallow enough for the rhino calf to touch bottom. It scampered out of the water while Dilly and I sunk down on the sand to rest. Swimming while guiding a baby rhino is as tiring as it sounds.

Led by a rope attached to Devi Kali's saddle, the calf walked all the way back to the stable between us. We had to trust Devi Kali to ward off any tigers up ahead that might want a chance to pounce on our rhino calf. To keep the calf calm, I talked to her.

Dilly shook his head and smiled. "You are a *shaman*, Nandu, just like *Subba-sahib*." My face flushed a little, but I kept talking to the rhino calf. I prayed to the gods that it might be true.

EIGHT

Drongos and barbets sang from their tree perches along our route home. Maybe the strange sight below them, an elephant leading two humans and a baby rhino, triggered the birds going off like alarms.

"*Subba-sahib*, look!" Ramji shouted to my father.

Devi Kali trumpeted, announcing our visitor. The calf ran up the flower-lined path, dragging the rope attached to the elephant. When the rope reached its end, the calf toppled over against the weight of Devi Kali.

"Nandu, I asked you and Dilly to bring back fish, and you brought back a rhino," my father said.

I untied Devi Kali from the rope. The freed rhino started running in circles, knocking over a bucket.

"*Subba-sahib*, we must go back to where we found her," Dilly said.

"The mother is dead, stuck in quicksand," I added. "Someone will steal the horn."

My father jumped up. "Why did not you say that right away?
Dilly, leave at once to call for the warden. Nandu, you must
show us where this happened. And, Ramji, five elephants, saddle
them now."

He turned to Rita. "Go borrow a bottle from Thakurdwara.
One that they use for the baby goats," he said. "And here are fifty
rupees for several quarts of buffalo milk. We will feed her some
to keep her happy."

The calf started bleating again. I did not want to leave her
side, especially to Rita.

"Don't worry, Nandu," said Rita. "I will watch over her while
you and Dilly are out. I will feed her." The rhino came up almost
to her elbows.

"Take good care of our new friend. She has no one in the
world now but us. I will be back very soon." I knew what it was
like to be abandoned in the jungle. I felt it almost every day of
my life.

Dilly had already returned with the warden. Below the
forest conservator-*sahib*, he was the highest ranking official in
the area, and just as lazy. But this news got him out of his ham-
mock. Rhinos belong to the king. There must be an inquest. And
failure to recover the precious horn and send it to the palace
could lead to his dismissal. His face was red, and it looked like

he had run all the way from his office, about five minutes' walk from Thakurdwara.

Both were still panting, the warden a bit more than Dilly. My father gave them a moment to catch their breath before we left.

Once across the river, Dilly and I led my father and the warden to the carcass. By now, dozens of vultures had started in on the dead rhino. Our arrival sent the scavengers back into the trees.

The warden slid down from his elephant to inspect the female rhino, writing everything in his book to send to the royal palace. We had to measure the rhino for his records. She was over ten feet long and must have weighed several tons. Ramji sawed off the horn; it was almost twenty inches, thick at the base and tapering to a sharp tip.

"We are lucky to have arrived in time, *Subba-sahib*," the warden said. "A horn this size is very valuable."

The drivers lashed ropes around the rhino. Pulling her from the quicksand took all five elephants straining together. Once the body was out of the muck, the warden instructed Ramji to remove the hooves and tail for the palace.

Our work was done.

When we returned to camp, I went straight to the cookhouse. Rita was resting against the mud wall with two empty baby bottles by her side. The calf had snuggled next to her with its head on her lap. It was snoring loudly.

I had never seen Rita look so happy.

"Nandu, we will call her Ritu."

"Yes, I like that name," I said. Not really, though.

I was jealous that she had taken my place so easily with the calf. But I knew I could not handle the calf on my own.

"She can sleep next to me in the cookhouse for tonight," Rita volunteered. "She must be so tired." She turned to the sleeping calf. "Ritu, I lost a parent, too. Do not worry. I will take care of you."

⌒

We put a cowbell around Ritu's neck so we could hear her if she ran off into the jungle. But we had no need to worry. The calf followed Rita everywhere. Rita was not allowed to be part of the stable staff, but my father gave her twenty rupees a week from his own pocket for tending to Ritu. He knew she would have done it for free, but my father wanted to encourage Rita's happiness, and perhaps be something of a father to her, too.

Under Rita's care, Ritu quickly became as tame as a baby goat. Well, an extremely large baby goat. By the fourth week, she was up to three quarts of buffalo milk each day, and "little" Ritu was not so little anymore; her gray, stout body had filled out fast, and she was eating the wild sugar cane that I cut for her from the jungle.

Rita and I would also take *baruwa* grass leaves and bundle

them with rice, molasses, and rock salt. These are the same *kuchi* treats we feed to our elephants. Except we made tiny *kuchis*, the size of my fist, for Ritu.

Now we just had to figure out what to do with her. If it was a male calf, my father said, we would have to give it up to the Kathmandu Zoo, because it needed a male, and a male would become too dangerous for us to keep after two years of age. But females are different, and Ritu had instantly become everyone's favorite—except for the elephants, who were not so fond of her.

Rita and I were leaning up against Tulsi's hut, with Ritu snuggled between us. My father approached us with a serious look on his face.

"I have received word from the warden."

Rita and I held our breath.

Subba-sahib broke into a smile. "Ritu can stay at the stable for now. After a few years she will likely find her way back into the jungle. But until then, she is our charge. Rita, you must take good care of her."

Rita's eyes watered, and we each wrapped our arms around Ritu, who snuggled in even closer between us.

"Nandu, I could not bear the thought of Ritu being taken away," Rita said. "Imagine if you would be separated from Devi Kali?"

When the days grow cool, it is time to head to the base of the mountains to collect the *babiyo* grass and wild cotton we use to make rope. The whole stable, all seventy-five men, were weaving fibers into ropes, singing while they worked.

The sound of an approaching jeep rumbled through the camp and silenced the singing. We never see jeeps or Land Rovers out here, except when the king and members of the royal family come to hunt.

The forest conservator-*sahib*, old Watermelon Belly, swung himself out of the car. We had not seen him since the king's visit many weeks earlier. I was sure he had not forgotten. And now the old drivers, who had barely started talking to me again, would be reminded, too.

My father rose to meet our guest. The official waddled toward us like a duck. His watermelon had grown even bigger and looked ready for harvest.

I grabbed the teapot from the edge of the firepit and poured the forest conservator-*sahib* a cup of our best black tea. He drank a bit and put down the glass. By his side was an envelope with a seal on it. He handed it to my father.

My father did not open it but sipped his tea instead.

"Excellent tea, by the way," said Watermelon Belly.

"The black pepper in it I picked only yesterday," my father said.

"*Subba-sahib*, if you do not open the envelope, I will open it for you. It is from the palace."

My father did not budge.

"Never mind, I have my own copy," said Watermelon Belly.

He pulled out a letter and handed it to my father, who had some trouble reading it because he had little schooling. My heart started to race in excitement. I was about to offer my father assistance, but then I thought I might embarrass him in front of the officer.

The forest conservator-*sahib* grew impatient.

"Nandu, read me the letter," *Subba-sahib* commanded and handed it to me. I do not think he trusted Watermelon Belly.

"What does it say, Nandu?" *Subba-sahib* asked. I studied the letter a moment before reading it aloud.

To the Senior Officer-in-Charge
of the Royal Elephant Stable,
Thakurdwara, the Borderlands:

The Palace Wildlife Committee, serving at the will of
His Majesty Birendra Bir Bikram Shah Dev, commands
the closing of the elephant stable in Thakurdwara. All
elephants, but one, and personnel are to be relocated
to the stable in Chitwan. From this day hence, all royal
hunts will occur in Chitwan. By January of next year, all
proceedings shall be completed. This it is written.

—The Honorable General K. S. Rana,
Secretary to His Majesty

The forest conservator-*sahib* broke in. "Here is how things stand," he began. "The royal family was disappointed that the king had no luck hunting tigers in the Borderlands. So they went to Chitwan just before *Tihar* and shot three in one day and five in the week they spent there. The hunting is better there, you see?"

My father said nothing. I cursed Watermelon Belly under my breath.

"The order has come to shut down this stable. The elephants will go to Chitwan, where the royal hunts will continue."

"I do not understand you," my father said, barely above a whisper.

"We are a poor country, *Subba-sahib*. We cannot afford to keep so many elephant stables. Out of respect for your services, the king will allow you to keep one elephant here for yourself, even against my advice to the Palace Wildlife Committee."

While Watermelon Belly spoke, my father stared at him as if the forest conservator-*sahib* were speaking a foreign language.

"So there are your orders. A little more than a year from now, on January first, this stable will be closed. Now you have a bit of time to get ready. The *Subba-sahib* in Chitwan still needs to build housing for your drivers and more stalls for your elephants. Then you will receive a final visit from me."

My father remained silent.

"I will lead the elephants to Chitwan, in time for the spring royal hunt. And you are to start the planning now." He looked around. "So finish making your new ropes. And lots of them. The *babiyo* is not so plentiful in Chitwan."

Before my father could respond, the forest conservator-*sahib* stood up and signaled his driver. When he turned to go, he added, "*Subba-sahib*, soon jeeps and Land Rovers will be everywhere in the Borderlands. We will not need elephant drivers out here. We will need mechanics. You might learn to be one."

As Watermelon Belly squeezed into his jeep and roared away, my father spat on the ground. He walked slowly back to his quarters, and I followed a bit behind him. I felt sick to my stomach with guilt and rage.

So this is what is meant by fate. What did I do? The other drivers were right. Why didn't I just shut my eyes like *Subba-sahib* told me to do?

"This is my fault, *Subba-sahib*. I ruined the king's hunt."

"This is not about the tigress, Nandu."

"But where will we go? They will take Devi Kali from me," I said. I could not help that words were tumbling from my mouth; my whole throat was burning. "Dilly will leave, and what about Tulsi and Rita? And Ritu! She is too young to be sent back into the jungle on her own."

"Do not worry, Nandu," my father said. "I will come up with a good plan. I will send word to His Majesty. I have connections, too. I still have a friend in the royal palace who looks favorably on us."

I wanted to believe that *Subba-sahib* could save the stable, that this was not the end for us, but Watermelon Belly had been so sure.

At first I was angry with my father that he had said nothing to Watermelon Belly. He had not defended our stable. But later that night, Ramji—who was the only driver not angry with me all over again—made me very proud of my father. Ramji said, "Nandu, your father may be just a lowly Tharu, but he is a *Subba-sahib*. He bows to no one but the king and queen."

NINE

want to be a dhole.

That is the thought that kept running through my head. *Dhole* have no masters, no Watermelon Bellies, no kings to tell them what to do and where to live. I wanted to run away. I was ashamed of the trouble I had caused. The older drivers did not have to say it to me. I could sense them whispering behind my back, "Nandu, he has brought bad luck to our stable."

I tried to pretend as if nothing had happened, as if their whispering did not matter—but it did.

My father sensed my despair. "Nandu, I will dictate a letter you must write out for me to the Palace Wildlife Committee," he said.

I wrote this as my father spoke it. He may have had no schooling, but in this moment his words flowed like a teacher's. Perhaps it was a bit of his *jhankri* magic.

To His Majesty and Your Graces,

We ask that you reconsider your plans to shut the Thakurdwara stable. The hunt was not successful this year, but I remind Your Graces that the Borderlands are home to the largest male tigers in the world. I have seen the tracks of several of them myself. I believe that they will surely make the finest trophies and break all records. We await your reply, remaining your humble servants.

—Kumar Lotan, Senior Officer-in-Charge,
Subba-sahib, Thakurdwara

After the letter was written, we set out on an overgrown trail, riding high on Devi Kali. The path was rough, and as we rocked from side to side, we had to hold our arms up to push the branches away from our faces. I let them slip through my hands as we moved, releasing each one just in time to shield my face from another. The rhythm put me in a kind of trance, but the sudden whistle of a wild dog pack snapped me back into the moment.

My father told Devi Kali to halt. A lone *dhole* ran through the forest ahead of us. Moments later, several others followed behind. They were on a hunt.

No one can track a wandering *dhole* pack. They zigzag back and forth across the Borderlands to chase the sambar deer and to keep far away from tigers. Next to elephants, they are my favorite animals.

"The *dhole* are like my brothers," I said.

"Yes," my father said. "The *dhole* have good hearts—at least when it comes to small children lost in the jungle. I would not want to be a young sambar around one."

"If the stable closes, *Subba-sahib*," I suddenly blurted, "I will go back into the jungle and live with the *dhole*."

My father turned to look me in the eye. "Do not worry, Nandu. I will not let them take this jungle life away from us. You and I are like the *dhole*; this is the only life we know. Besides, I have tamed you now. There is no going back."

I smiled at my father's joke as he slipped down off Devi Kali to pick up some large round pellets.

"Which type of deer left this?"

"That is the sambar," I said. "The biggest deer in the jungle and the tiger's favorite."

"Very good. Now what are the others that the tiger hunts?"

"Spotted deer, hog deer, swamp deer, and barking deer, and when he can catch one, wild boar."

Just then, a large animal ran across the grassland.

"Look, a *nilgai* male," *Subba-sahib* whispered.

"His long nose and mane always reminds me of a horse. I would like to break one and try to ride it like Devi Kali," I said.

"Ha! The *nilgai* would never let you. Not all animals are as gracious as the elephant. In fact, I cannot think of one more generous."

As if joining into our conversation, Devi Kali rumbled. In fact, she must have been talking to us, because there were no other elephants for her to rumble to.

"Devi Kali, I will ride you forever and ever," I patted her. "I did not mean what I said about the *nilgai*."

Then my father said, "Nandu, I have something to tell you."

His tone made my body go tight.

"Your future is very important to me."

He paused.

"There is no easy way to say it. I have enrolled you in the certificate school in Gularia."

My heart started pounding, and my head felt like it was coming off. I could not believe that my father was sending me away to boarding school. Maybe the other drivers told him to send me somewhere far from the stable.

"No, *Subba-sahib*! You just said that you and I are like the *dhole*! We cannot live any other way."

"It is not forever, Nandu. You will get your certificate. It will take only two years, and at the end you will be qualified for many positions. I do not have any intention of letting the stable close."

"I know you will do what you can, but the forest conservator-*sahib* seemed so sure of the king's word."

"I have greater faith in my own powers," he said. "But that

is not for you to worry about. This is the perfect time for you to go and learn more than Tulsi can ever teach you. You must leave this week to make the opening of the winter term."

I knew Gularia was the district capital, twenty-five miles away, but I had never been there. I had only heard the dirt streets were muddy, the water smelled like dead fish, and rats were everywhere. It was as filthy as my jungle is clean and beautiful. How would I survive there, far from Devi Kali, my father, and Dilly?

"*Subba-sahib*, I cannot leave this week. It is impossible." Now I saw his plan. He had deliberately waited until five days before the term started to tell me. Maybe he thought if he told me earlier I would have run off with Devi Kali and never returned. He had betrayed me.

I could feel my father smiling, even though I could not see his face.

"Boarders, as you will be, can come home for a week-long break at the end of every two months in the school year. And then there is the three-month break from May until August."

I looked down at the saddle. "I cannot live in Gularia, *Subba-sahib*, please. I will die without Devi Kali." I hesitated. "And without you."

For once, my father had no answer. Instead he made a low whistle and pointed across the river, where the langur monkeys were leaping in the giant fig trees on the other bank. We watched in silence as they scampered along the branches and chased one another.

I was the first to speak. "*Subba-sahib*, don't you see how happy they are in the trees with their families? Why do you want to throw me out into the world?"

"Nandu," my father said, "you must listen to me for I have lived long and can see ahead. The Borderlands are changing. You must go to school and gain knowledge and skills that I do not have. For this stable to survive, I have to find someone to lead it when I am too old to do so. Someone who can guide the drivers, not just to identify tracks and avoid the quicksand along the river, but guide them in a world that is very different from the one in which I grew up. I see no one but you capable of this task."

Across the river, the langur monkeys were still playing chase, stopping abruptly now and then to pluck a ripe fig. Underneath them, a herd of spotted deer waited for the monkeys to discard some fruit. A stork-billed kingfisher started to wail along the riverbank.

It was hard to imagine, but I knew in this moment it was true. Life in the jungle would go on without me. But how would I go on without it?

PART II

A MAHOUT'S EDUCATION

TEN

Not until the oxcart was loaded with my belongings and rolling away, did I dare to look back. My father stood by the gate, waving. Beyond him lay the stable, the drivers' barracks, the tethering area for the elephants, the gazebo near the fire pit, and my father's bungalow. This place was my only home. In a year, for all I knew, there might be only a tangle of morning glory and wild cucumber vines where there once was a stable. I could not even be sure my father would be alive.

Rita ran up beside the oxcart and waved to me, with little Ritu running alongside her, clanging her cowbell. I waved back, but I could not look toward the elephants. I could not face saying good-bye to Devi Kali.

I held on to my tears until no one could see me. I was facing backward, to Thakurdwara. The smoke plume from the burning elephant dung rising from the stable grew smaller and smaller as we moved down the dirt track.

And then I saw them, six bright red dogs—the *dhole*—trotting down the trail. It seemed like they, too, were saying good-bye, making sure one last time, maybe, that I was safe. I waved to the leader, and they all stopped and stared at me then darted into the forest.

They had stayed with me as long as they could—just like when I was a baby. But I was not a *dhole*, I was not a regular boy, either. Now, away from my father and Devi Kali, I had no idea who I was.

Hours later, we rolled up to the school and Dilly and Ramji helped me unload. I barely had time to say good-bye. The hall master approached and led me to a changing room so I could put on my new uniform—a white shirt and blue pants. Tulsi had sewn them for me just before I left. This was to be what I wore while at Future Scholars Boarding School.

The evening meal was about to be served and now I faced another pack of dogs: a room full of boys. I was standing in front of my new classmates in the dining hall, waiting to be introduced by the hall master.

As I scanned their faces, I hoped, now that I was out of Thakurdwara and the Borderlands, there might be others who looked like me. But these were all light-skinned, high-caste boys. A sea of them. There were no familiar round-faced Tharu with dark skin, or a Tamang with almond eyes, like Dilly. There was no one who looked even remotely like me—tall, straight dark hair, high cheekbones and reddish-brown skin. As I stood, gazing around the room, the boys eyed me back suspiciously. They probably thought I was a yak herder separated from his caravan.

Before dinner began, the hall master of our dormitory announced, "Please, everyone, welcome Nanda Singh from the Thakurdwara elephant stable, your new classmate and our new scholar."

That was it for introductions. The hall master had already turned his back and walked out of the cafeteria with another staff member. The adults were gone. My ears started burning when all forty boys on the benches began whistling and hissing at me like cobras. The room smelled like kerosene and sweat. I could not run. I had to sit down and join them.

I found an empty space on a bench. I kept my head down and started eating. I had a powerful thirst. Reaching for my water glass, I accidentally sent it flying and spilled water all over the boy sitting across from me.

He gasped, and before I could apologize, he roused the others to his side.

"Look at the copperhead that slithered out from an elephant stable." The boy's nose looked like the beak of a griffon vulture. *Vulture Face*, I said to myself, *leave me alone*.

"Copperhead, Copperhead," he chanted and the other boys joined in.

I shot Vulture Face a look to keep quiet.

"What are you staring at, butt-face?" he snarled at me.

"Quiet!" The hall master shouted, annoyed, running back in to see what had happened.

The boys stopped taunting me then, but it was only temporary. I knew there was no one, no rule that could make them act friendly toward me.

Before class began the next morning, I went out to the playing field, looking for birds. A group of boys, led by Vulture Face, found me and began chucking half-dried cow turds and empty plastic water bottles at me.

I stood still—I would not run from them.

My new white shirt was soon spotted with brown stains. When the bell rang for class, the boys raced into the school. I ran to the edge of the forest and tried to wash my shirt in the stream. Luckily, I saw a *chiuri* tree and grabbed a few ripe fruits to squeeze out the juice to make soap, the way Tulsi had taught me.

This is my fate. Wherever I go, I will never fit in.

I was ten minutes late when I arrived breathlessly into the math room. The rest of the students were already seated. I slid along a wooden bench in the back and kept my eyes on the desk in front of me, hoping that no one would say anything about my wet shirt.

When I finally looked up, I saw the teacher. He was a sight I had never seen before—a white man. I wondered if he looked like the British scientist my father had met so many years ago. Even more strange was that he was not even really white. He had pink skin, white hair, and a dark black coat with a white collar that peeked out at his throat like a tiny window.

"Who is the late arrival?" the teacher asked. I could not believe he spoke Nepali.

I stood up immediately and bowed. "Nanda Singh, sir."

"Take your seat please, Mr. Nanda Singh."

The other students tittered.

"I am your new teacher, Father Robert Autry," the tall pink man said, staring straight at me. "I will teach you English, reading, math, and science. If you do your work and pay attention, I will turn all of you into true scholars. You will be better educated than the most privileged children in Kathmandu."

This Father Robert Autry, he not only spoke Nepali, but he spoke it like the king! Perfect, every word, with no accent.

"I am retired," Father Autry continued, "but my former student from Saint Xavier's, in the capital, is your headmaster, and he asked me to teach just this one semester. I am delighted to be here, and I know you will make much progress in the four months I am with you.

"I am also hoping that you can help me make progress with my studies as well. I am a student of nature, of animals, plants, birds, and I have not yet spent much time in southern Nepal. I would like more than anything to see a tiger in the wild. I have lived in Nepal for twenty years and never seen one."

I shot up from my seat. "I can show you a tiger, Master-*sahib*," I nearly shouted. All my classmates turned to give me a smirk.

"Thank you, Mr. Nanda Singh. That would be most excellent."

Father Autry then gave me the kindest smile I had seen since I came to Gularia.

"Now, class," he said, "enough about me. Let us turn to today's math lesson."

My ears burned as I stood there. I had twice made a fool of myself on the first day, with our new teacher and in front of all of my classmates.

I sat down on my bench and opened my math book. The problems in the lesson did not seem hard at all. Tulsi had taught me to divide and multiply two years ago, using the elephant's *kuchis*. "Now, Nandu and Rita," she would say, "if we do not get these answers right, the elephants will not get their fair share of *kuchis* and they will go hungry. We would not want that, would we?" Rita and I worked hard to learn quickly and get the correct answers. Tulsi knew that nothing would motivate us more than our love for the elephants.

Suddenly, I felt eyes looking over my shoulder. "Psst, Copperhead, what is sixteen divided by four?"

"Leave me alone," I said shaking my head.

The boy glared back at me. Vulture Face, who was in the row ahead of me, heard us and turned around and whispered, "Tell him the answer now, or I will stuff elephant turds in your schoolbag."

"Four, and do not bother me again."

"Is there a conversation I need to be part of, Nanda Singh?"

"No, Master-*sahib*," I replied standing up.

At least *he* did not call me Copperhead. I had heard about how mean the high-caste boys could be to dark-skinned boys, or any boy who was not Hindu. I did not know what I was: Buddhist, like the red string necklace said I was; Hindu, like all of these boys; or animist, like my father. I really did not care about castes and skin color or religion. I loved the jungle, Devi Kali, and the laws of nature, which were sometimes harsh, like when the leopard killed the dancing peacock, but they were never mean. These students were awful, worse even than king cobras.

How would I survive here?

I thought seriously about running away. It was not the challenge of the schoolwork. I could keep up just fine, even though I could only speak a few sentences of English. Most of the students in my class were weak in English, too. No, I wanted to leave because I did not belong here. I was born to wake up and see my elephant tethered across from me. I was born to live in the jungle. Perhaps that is why I was found there. Perhaps they should have left me there.

On my second week at school, during the last class of the afternoon, Father Autry asked us to shut our books and answer three questions.

"Class, who can tell me the sum of forty-nine plus twenty-seven?"

No one said anything but simply went to work with their

pencils on the lined paper. I imagined forty-nine *kuchis* in one pile for Devi Kali and twenty-seven *kuchis* for Man Kali, like Tulsi had taught us. Without thinking, I raised my hand.

"Yes, Nanda?"

"Sir, I believe the answer is seventy-six *kuchis*, I mean, seventy-six."

"Very good."

Vulture Face shot me a look of disgust. Vulture Face's real name was Gopal Mishra, and he was a priest-caste Brahmin, the highest caste in Nepal.

"Here is a tricky one. Who can tell me what is four times four times four divided by four?"

Again, my classmates worked their numbers. I imagined how to divide up the *kuchis* among four of our elephants.

I raised my hand.

"Yes, Nanda. Do you want me to repeat the question for you?"

"No, sir. The answer is sixteen."

"Yes, that is correct." Everyone turned to look at me.

"Now, class, here is the really hard one. I will write it on the board. Even my students in Kathmandu failed to get this right the first time. What is nine plus eleven plus five, divided by five, then multiplied by one hundred?"

This time I imagined the numbers like strands of *babiyo* grass I had to weave together. This is how Tulsi had taught Rita and me multiplication and division. I raised my hand again.

"Sir, I believe Nanda has to go to the bathroom," said Gopal. The other students laughed.

"The answer is five hundred," I said.

"Excellent, Nanda."

Another boy let out a soft whistle and whispered to Gopal, "Maybe you should let Nanda tutor you." Everyone laughed at his joke, except for me—and Vulture Face.

I grew more confident until I had to take the first school test of my life. My knees knocked against the legs of the desk. I watched Father Autry write the exam questions on the blackboard. There were ten problems: some addition, some subtraction, some division, and some multiplication. The last two combined several operations. We were to copy the problems in our notebook, then solve them.

As I wrote each one down, I found myself making the equals sign and then writing the answer before Father Autry had started writing the next problem on the blackboard. The numbers joined in my mind; I did not have to line them up in a column.

Father Autry finished writing the problem set on the blackboard and sat down to monitor us. He saw me look up at him while the other students were head down in their notebooks.

"Is there a problem, Nanda Singh?"

"No, sir. Excuse me, sir, but I have finished."

I saw Vulture Face's mouth open, and he made a sound like all the air had escaped his body.

I got up and handed in my notebook, and Father Autry looked over my answers.

"I am stunned, Nanda. You are either a wizard or a prodigy, and I do not believe in wizards. You have earned an early exit from class today. Go enjoy your Friday afternoon. I will see you on Monday."

I floated down the hallway. The famous educator from Kathmandu had called me a prodigy. Instead of heading back to my room, I crossed the playing field and walked into the next building. A carved wood sign at the entrance said LIBRARY.

I had never been in a library or even seen a picture of one. There were shelves of books everywhere. Some were in Nepali, but most were in English. On a shelf labeled ANIMALS I found about a dozen volumes. The one that caught my eye had a red binding, *The Jungle Book*. I took it down and found a table where I could sit and read. It was so quiet my footsteps creaked across the wooden floor.

Mixed in with the text were drawings of animals I already knew. I started to read the first few pages. The English was difficult, but I was relieved to find it was about a young boy who talked to wild animals, just like I do. And he was raised by wolves. I began to feel like the book was written about me.

I took the book back to my tiny room and read until the morning light came through the window shutters, using the going-away gift from Tulsi, Rita, and Dilly—an English dictionary.

Maybe I did not have a single friend at school, but at least now I had Mowgli and his friends in *The Jungle Book*.

I could hear mynas and parakeets outside the library window on my daily visits, but I never went outside to look. Inside I was safe, the high-castes never set foot in this room. The walls of books made it feel crowded and dense like the jungle. I loved to climb the ladder to the top shelf, like I climbed trees back home. If only there were monkeys sitting at the top eating figs. I laughed aloud at this thought and startled myself, when my voice echoed in the empty room.

Among the books about animals was one about the rhinos in Sumatra. They are small and hairy like coconut shells. And there are so few of them left. I read how hunters catch them by digging pits in the ground along the rhino trails. They cover the pit with sticks and leaves so the rhino falls into it.

After the library closed, I would return to my room and read there until dinner. My room was really no more than a large closet. It barely had enough space for my cot and a small table. I had a tiny window at one end. On the wall was a calendar. I crossed off the days of each week, counting down to the start of my first break.

When I reached four weeks, I put a double-X through each day on the calendar. *One month to go.*

ELEVEN

I had been packed and ready to leave two days before January
20th, the day Ramji and Dilly were to come and fetch me. I
was waiting by the tea stalls in the small bazaar down below
the school. Any minute now, Dilly and Ramji would roll down
the dusty track in the oxcart.

I had nothing to do, so I started counting the metallic-green
flies landing on the plate of *samosas* and *chapaties* for sale. I stopped
counting at two hundred. Gularia was swarming with flies and
scorpions. Even the coldest day of winter could not keep them
away. Finally, I saw the oxcart, a smiling Dilly, a frowning Ramji.
I jumped up from where I was sitting and waved.

During the six-hour drive back to Thakurdwara, they told
me about all that had happened at the stable while I was gone.

The most exciting news was that Rita was now in charge of
another baby rhino. A two month old calf had become separated
from her mother. The calf had escaped a tiger trying to kill it,

but was covered in claw marks and bites when they found her. "You know what *Subba-sahib* says," Ramji added. " 'If you live next to a wild jungle like the Borderlands, there will be plenty of orphaned animals.' "

"Like you," Dilly interrupted, punching my arm. A punch never felt so good.

As we headed onto the final stretch of dirt road before the elephant stable, a small cloud of dust rolled toward us. Above the cloud was the flying long black hair of Rita. Just behind her was a bigger cloud kicked up by Ritu, who had grown to be half as tall as Rita but still followed her like a baby.

"Nandu!" she called. "You are home!"

When we drew closer to her, I jumped down and gave her a hug. I never thought I would be so happy to see Rita. I walked the rest of the way to the stable with her. She chattered away like the solo jungle babbler she is, telling me about the new calf and about how my father had saved it from dying. They had named the calf Rona.

My father was walking quickly toward us—as quickly as he could with his gout. He greeted me warmly, pulling me close, just for an instant. I had waited so long to ask my father for any news about the stable, I blurted out, "*Subba-sahib*, do you have any news from the palace?"

"I have heard from my contact, but these things take time. Nothing happens fast in Nepal, Nandu," he said. "There could be many delays, or they could lack the funds to build new stables in

Chitwan for our elephants. In the meantime, they could change their minds. Now, if you are not busy, Devi Kali needs some exercise. She grew very lazy while you were gone."

"I am going, *Subba-sahib!*" I yelled, unable to surpress my smile, as I ran for the clearing, where I could see Devi Kali waiting for me.

Dilly ran after me. "Wait up, Nandu, I am coming with you."

Dilly let me sit in front, and as we rode through the jungle, I rubbed Devi Kali between her ears. She rumbled, letting me know that she was just as happy to see me. The star-shaped flowers of the wild coffee had begun to bloom across the forest floor, like an endless carpet of white. And so fragrant, nothing like the kerosene and sweat and stale urine smells from the dormitory I had just left behind.

I knew then that I could never return to school. I was determined to persuade my father that I was already smart enough to do the books and run the stable. After all, Father Autry had called me a prodigy.

When we reached the base of the hillside where the *babiyo* grows, Devi Kali bent her front legs and let me walk over her head. Then she lowered me to the ground just the way she did when I was a little boy. After she stood again, I hugged her trunk, then watched her wander off to graze while Dilly and I cut grass.

Dilly shook his head. "You really are a jungle boy, Nandu."

"It is true!" I said, laughing.

As we worked cutting the grass, my arms grew tired. In such

a short time, I was already growing weak from sitting in class.

"Dilly," I said. "I am not returning to boarding school."

Dilly stopped working and rested his forearm against a tree. For once, he looked quite serious. "What are you saying, Nandu? That is not for you to decide."

"It is my life. And there is no reason for me to be there. I thought maybe there would be other boys like me. But nobody looks like me. I thought maybe I would learn something about my people. But I have only learned that I am as good at math as Tulsi always told me. And I am more lonely than I have ever been in all my life."

Instead of making a joke, like I thought he would, Dilly pointed to the ridge above the lake and motioned for me to climb it with him. "Come on, let's run to the top. If we take a quick look and race down, we will be back in time to ride to the stable before dark."

"I will beat you to the top!" I shouted. I let out all my feelings by running as hard as I could up the mountain. I was a hundred feet ahead of Dilly when I reached the ridgeline.

I stopped and bent over to catch my breath. I was covered in sweat. Dilly caught up and stood by my side, panting heavily. In a few minutes, the cool breezes blowing through the pine forest had dried us off. The air was so fresh, and the fallen pine needles made the ground soft under our feet. It felt like a new world, high above the hot steamy lowlands.

I had never been up on the ridge before. It was the highest

point in the Borderlands, and from there, the drivers said, you could see India.

"Come on, Nandu, there is a great view over here through this clearing," said Dilly.

I followed him to an opening in the forest, but instead of looking south to India, he pointed north. For the first time in my life, I saw the snow peaks of the Himalayas. Their tops gleamed in the bright sunlight. My lungs filled with pine scent and my eyes could barely take it all in.

"That is where your people come from," said Dilly. "Your skin color is the same as the tribesmen of the Himalayas and the Tibetans to the north of the mountains. Now turn around and look south."

Below us was a sweeping view of the Borderlands. We could see the broad flood plain of the Great Sand Bar River that flowed toward India, where it joined the Ganges. To the east, we saw the Babai River cutting the Borderlands in two. And in between, a bright green blanket, the wildest jungle on Earth. My jungle.

"Now, Nandu, how do you think you came to be a baby walking around down here, when your people live so far away?"

I had no answer.

"There are things we do not know about our fate. Things no one can ever answer. But we have to trust that the world is showing us the way. My father told me that *Subba-sahib* is closer to the gods than an ordinary man. He found you, or you found him. Either way, you must respect what the gods have in store for you.

You must take your guidance from him. If he were my father, I would be so honored, Nandu. I wish I had the brains to go to Future Scholars, but I do not. That is not my path, but it is yours."

I had never heard Dilly talk this way. He was not angry, but he was serious and his eyes filled with tears.

"I thought *Subba-sahib* was sending me away because"—my voice started to tremble—"because the drivers blame me for the closing of the stable. When the king could not shoot the tigress because I scared it away."

"Nandu, maybe some of them blame you, the foolish ones and the old farts unable to think for themselves. They will come around. I do not blame you and neither does Ramji. I blame the forest conservator-*sahib* for not standing up for us."

"But what if I want to sweep up elephant dung all my life? What if the *Subba-sahib* is wrong and that is my destiny, truly."

"Then you are less of a magician than I thought!" Dilly exclaimed, shooting me one of his grins before taking off down the mountain.

"Not fair," I called. "You got a head start!"

I ran after him as hard as I could, feeling like he was the closest thing I had to a brother. Maybe I should listen to him and let fate be my guide. Maybe something would happen while I was home, something that would make it clear that I must never go back to Gularia.

Later, my father and I sat around the campfire, drinking tea. He asked me to tell stories about school, so I told him how I finished my exam so quickly I got to take the afternoon off.

"Show me your marks," my father said.

When I did, he slapped his hand on his thigh and laughed. "I knew you were meant to go to school," he said, "but this is more than I ever imagined you could do."

"My teacher, Father Autry, called me a prodigy," I said, not able to help enjoying my father's praise.

"What does this mean, 'prodigy'?"

"It is an English word, *Subba-sahib*. I think it means a student who is quick with numbers." I could not hold back my true feelings, though, and added, "But I am happy to be home, *Subba-sahib*. I have no desire to go back to that awful school."

"But you performed so well on your test?"

"The school work is not the reason. The other boys are nasty to me, and I am miserable there."

My father's face grew angry, like when he once yelled at a driver for hitting his elephant with a stick. "What do you mean nasty?"

"They call me Copperhead and throw cow dung at me."

My father did not speak for a long time. I could tell a story was coming.

"Nandu, here at the stable, as long as I have been *Subba-sahib*, we do not judge our drivers by the color of their skin or their caste. You either are a skilled driver or you are not."

I did not look him in the face.

"You will be a great driver someday," he continued. "I am sure of it. But a great driver must sometimes absorb insults from the tongues of the royal family and officials from the higher castes and never talk back."

"You mean like the forest conservator-*sahib*?"

"Especially him, Nandu. For the cost of revealing your anger and embarrassing a Royal or the forest conservator-*sahib* is dismissal from the stable. And you would not want that."

I shook my head. "That is why you did not curse in public at the forest conservator-*sahib* when he told you and the drivers to become mechanics."

"That is correct, Nandu, I had to hold back to save our stable. Think of the insults of those boys at your school as training for your path to becoming a head driver."

And then he added, "Let me share with you a secret. But you must promise to tell no one."

"Yes, *Subba-sahib*," I replied.

"Every time they call you a name, you must say to yourself, 'I am Nanda Singh, the bravest elephant driver in Nepal.'"

I nodded.

"And then only to yourself, never out loud, you may say that this person is an elephant's ass."

I laughed—and so did my father.

"Now come, Nandu. Let us give Devi Kali her *kuchis*. She has been waiting patiently for her prodigy to feed her."

TWELVE

Fate did nothing during my first school break, except send me back to Future Scholars at the end of the week. But being home had lifted my spirits. I decided that I would think of school only as training to someday become *Subba-sahib* of our stable, which my father would surely save. And there was at least one person I was happy to see when I returned to school—Father Autry. After class my first day back, he asked me to stay to speak with him.

"Nanda, you are learning English faster than any of your classmates. How many languages do you speak?"

"Every child of the Borderlands speaks Nepali and Hindi, Father-*sahib*. And I speak Tharu with the drivers, and I know some Tamang because Dilly, Tulsi, and Rita speak it. Dilly is my best friend, Tulsi is his mother, and Rita is his sister."

"And at this rate, you will soon master English," he said. "There is a book I think you might enjoy reading. It is a famous story that introduced me to the animals of Nepal. It is called *The Jungle Book.* And I suspect you will like it. It is about a boy like you."

Father Autry handed me the book, and I bowed. "Thank you, Father-*sahib.* I will start reading tonight." I thought about telling him that I had already read it three times. I also wanted to tell him that I was a *real* jungle boy, protected by wild dogs until my father found me. But I did not want to seem rude.

Then I had a brilliant thought. Maybe at my next school break, Father Autry could come to the stable with me and let me show him the jungle. I tried to speak, but I lacked the courage. I turned to leave, then turned back around.

"Yes, Nanda?"

"Father-*sahib,* would you like to see a tiger from the top of an elephant? I would be so pleased to show you, if you would be our guest in Thakurdwara."

"What a wonderful invitation. I would be most honored to accompany you to your home during the next holiday."

"Oh that is great, Father-*sahib.* My father would be so happy to meet you, too."

Without thinking, I ran out of the schoolroom. I would have to send a message to my father right away so he could prepare for my teacher's visit.

That week I was also lucky to move into a bigger room with windows in the student dorm. The boy I was replacing had gone back home, claiming homesickness.

"I do not have homesickness," I told my new roommate, Ballam Abdullah, "I have elephant-sickness. I cannot wait for the summer break to come." He was also a Thakurdwara boy, and he understood me. He was the youngest of five sons born to the local carpenter, Hassan Abdullah. Every one in Thakurdwara and the villages knew Hassan Abdullah because he built their furniture. But I had only met Ballam once or twice before. His father had sent him off to Future Scholars when Ballam was only six years old.

Living with Ballam I quickly learned that I was not a prodigy after all. Ballam was the real one, not me. After only a few weeks of sharing a room with him, he began tutoring me. He was the smartest in our class, and he was also the smallest.

They called him Dwarf.

I was called other things, but never Dwarf. I was already a head taller than the other boys my age. And I was stronger than everyone, even the older students. I guess all those years of cutting thousands of bundles of wild sugar cane and tossing them up on the backs of elephants had made my muscles more powerful than I knew.

Ballam soon became my friend, a true friend. Besides doing our math and English homework together, he also taught me some basic Urdu and to read and write the swirling script. The letters seemed alive to me.

We would lie awake at night and tell each other stories.

When it was my turn, I would tell him about the jungle and about Devi Kali. He loved to hear me tell about the hand ax and how I saved Chuchi.

One evening I finally told him the story of being guarded by the *dhole* and then being discovered by Devi Kali and the man who became my father. Ballam did not try to guess why the *dhole* chose to spare me. But when I mentioned that they found me with the red strings of a Buddhist tied around my neck, he sat up. He had learned about other religious customs, Hindu, Buddhist, and animist. He was also a devout Muslim and prayed five times a day.

"Nandu," he asked me earnestly, "do you believe in God?"

I thought about it and said, "I guess I am closest to animist. Sometimes I watch my father go into a trance when he prays to the forest goddess, Ban Devi. She is one I know who watches over us."

"I hear she is a very powerful goddess," Ballam said, as if she were someone who lived in our village. He paused. "Nandu, do you believe there is a heaven?"

I did not hesitate this time. "Yes, Ballam. And I imagine it filled with the animals I love. But in this heaven, the tiger no longer kills the sambar, and the monkeys have no fear of eagles carrying off their young. Even the peacocks strut and dance in peace. The sloth bear leaves the honeycomb for the bees. In my heaven, Ballam, the animals do not eat one another. Even the king cobra is peaceful and never bites an elephant." I paused, to imagine such a place where no creature ever dies. "In my heaven, I ride Devi Kali forever."

Ballam was quiet, and I was, too.

"Can I ask you something else?" said Ballam. I could tell we were finally getting around to what was really on his mind.

"Why do the other boys mock me about my religion, while you are so kind to me?"

"Who makes fun of you, Ballam?"

"I do not want to say, but they call me towel head, and worse things. And when I pray outside, they throw cow turds at me and the other Muslim students."

"Who are they? Tell me their names," I said.

"Please do not say I told you?"

"Never."

Ballam named the two leaders. One was Gopal Mishra, of course. The other was Raj Kumar Oli.

And then I repeated to my friend what the *Subba-sahib* had taught me.

"Every time they mock you, you must say to yourself, 'I am Ballam Abdullah, and I am the smartest boy in the Borderlands.' You must never curse back at them. Do you understand me, Ballam?"

"Yes, Nandu."

My kerosene lantern was still lit, and Ballam stared intently at my face. I tried to look as serious as possible.

"And then, only to yourself, never out loud, you may say that this person is an elephant's ass."

I could not keep back my smile any longer. We both started laughing like hyenas.

Finally, Ballam blew out the lantern and we lay quietly. Outside the window, I heard the knocking song of a nightjar.

"Gopal Mishra is an elephant's ass," I said into the darkness.

"Raj Kumar Oli is an elephant's ass," Ballam said in return. We kept at it, more and more time passing between turns, until finally we fell asleep.

The next day, I kept an eye on Gopal and Raj Kumar. I followed them to the area where Ballam and a few other Muslim students were kneeling on their carpets in prayer. Gopal and Raj Kumar picked up some dried cow turds and began tossing them at the students.

When the two headed back to their room, I was waiting.

I grabbed both of them and pinned them against the wall. I could not believe my own strength or the depth of my anger. All of the insults from the past three months and all of my despair at being an outsider took over my body.

"If you ever throw anything at my friend again or say one more insulting word to him, I will beat you both." It was the first time in my life I had ever threatened anyone.

Their faces were starting to turn bright red. A pool of urine puddled under Gopal's bare feet.

"Do you understand me?"

Raj Kumar had begun to whimper. They both nodded, and I let them go.

Suddenly, I realized that, if they told the principal, I might be thrown out of school. My father would be very angry with me, and Father Autry would cancel his visit.

"If you ever tell anyone what just happened, I will leave cobras and kraits in your beds."

That was the last time anyone at school bothered Ballam. And I never heard the name Copperhead again.

These boys were in all ways inferior to Ballam and me, except by caste. Yet, I had done exactly what my father had warned me not to do. I practiced what I would say, should the worst happen. "Forgive me, *Subba-sahib*, but I have learned that saying to yourself so-and-so is an elephant's ass is sometimes not enough."

THIRTEEN

It was finally spring and the branches of the silk cotton tree in the middle of the school grounds were filled with bright red flowers—and parakeets, barbets, sunbirds, and leafbirds.

I missed riding on Devi Kali in the great savanna across the Belgadi with the trees in bloom. I could not wait for our week's break in March, when Father Autry would visit the Borderlands. He would see my groves of silk cotton, not just one lonely tree in a courtyard.

My father had arranged with the warden for Father-*sahib* to stay at the rest house next to his compound. Even the warden was impressed that we were hosting a Western guest.

I arrived home first, again driven by Dilly and Ramji in the oxcart. Father Autry had some work to finish, so he left Gularia two days after me. When at last he arrived in his Land Rover, with his driver, Syam Lal, and cook, Dahan Bahadur, the entire staff stood in a circle near the entrance of camp to give him an honorable welcome.

To me, this was more exciting than the arrival of the king.

Father Autry stepped carefully down from the dusty vehicle, and I ran to his side. "Welcome, Father-*sahib*! This is my home, and I hope you will feel during your visit that it is yours, too!"

"Thank you, Nanda."

I led him first to meet my father. "*Subba-sahib*, this is my teacher, Father Autry-*sahib*. He has come to the jungle to photograph a tiger."

"I bow to the God in you, sir. I am very happy to meet you," Father Autry said.

I could see *Subba-sahib* hiding his smile. My teacher had greeted him using the most formal Nepali, which is reserved for the highest caste.

"*Namaste*, Father-*sahib*, we are so pleased you could come," my father replied. "Let us have some tea together before you retire to your cottage. You must be tired from your journey—"

"Oh I am not tired at all, *Subba-sahib*," Father Autry interrupted. "I am quite ready to head off into the jungle right away, if it is all the same to you. Though some tea would be wonderful."

"Of course," my father said, impressed with Father-*sahib*'s enthusiasm. He turned to Dilly and Ramji. "Saddle up three elephants and prepare to depart shortly."

As my father led Father Autry through the camp, I followed

close enough behind to listen. "I hope you know, sir," Father Autry said, "that Nanda is my prize student."

My father stopped to look at my teacher, his face beaming.

"I am grateful for your good teaching," my father said. Then he paused to find the right words. "I know you are anxious to see a tiger, Father-*sahib*, but I cannot promise you one now. They are smart and know how to hide. But let us see what we can find across the Belgadi River. I have heard the spotted deer barking since this morning, so there might be a cat moving around nearby. Maybe it is only a leopard. Would that suit you?"

"Oh yes, *Subba-sahib*. I have been here four months now in Gularia and have yet to set foot in the real jungle. I would be thrilled to see anything that jumps out at us!"

"Father-*sahib*, *Subba-sahib* is very skilled. He can call in a leopard with the sound of his voice," I offered.

Father Autry turned his head, "I believe you, Nanda. This is all very exciting!"

We had arrived at the other end of camp, where the elephants stood eating hay and occasionally throwing it over their heads, as if they were having their own little party.

"Ah, the elephants," said Father Autry. "Magnificent!"

My father motioned for me to gather the hot and steaming tea tray from one of the drivers who had brought it from the canteen. I offered Father Autry a cup of tea. "Here is your tea, Father-*sahib*. We can all drink while the drivers saddle the elephants, then we will be on our way."

I called out to Dilly, who was saddling Man Kali, asking him to come meet Father Autry. I wanted my teacher to know everyone close to me in my life. Just then, as if proving her worth, too, Ritu came barreling down the path, her cowbell clanging. Rita was running behind her, trying to grab the rope around her neck. I made the bleating sound I had used when Ritu was just a baby, and she ran right to me, stopping with a very loud clang of her bell.

"Oh my Lord!" said Father Autry.

"You can pet her," I said. "She is very tame."

Father Autry carefully ran his hand over her thick skin and the folds on her back. She turned and tried to grab his finger with her upper lip.

"Where did you find her, Nanda?"

"She found us, Father-*sahib*. I will tell you the story later. This is Rita, Dilly's sister. She takes care of Ritu. Rita, this is my teacher, Father Autry-*sahib*."

I was not sure if Rita would be jealous of my guest and teacher. But she bowed and made the *namaste* gesture. Ritu kept trying to grab Father Autry's finger.

"Look at her prehensile upper lip. Is it not a wonder? You know many ancient mammals used to have lips that they could project outward. The lips of our kind were not so common. This is very important for our lesson on mammals—"

But Father was interrupted, when the other young calf, who had survived the tiger attack, crashed into our group.

"Father-*sahib*, this is Rona," Rita said. "She wants your attention, too. She was abandoned by her mother, we do not know why, and then attacked by a tiger. I am caring for both of them." Rita was trying to impress my teacher. I could tell.

"A noble calling. They are obviously flourishing under your care."

Rita filled with pride. But I did not want her to horn in. Fortunately, she had to run off after Ritu and Rona, who had taken off toward the cookhouse.

Just before we boarded Bhim Prashad, I thought to ask, "Father-*sahib*, have you ever ridden on an elephant before?"

"Horses, many times. A camel once, even an ostrich, but never an elephant."

My father walked Bhim Prashad to the loading platform where my teacher could climb the stairs, then step off the platform onto the saddle. This was the easiest way for guests of the stable to get on. Soon we were ready to go. Next to us was Ramji on Devi Kali and Dilly on Man Kali. I sat in front of my father, and Father Autry sat behind him on the saddle holding his camera.

"How different the world looks from up here on an elephant's back," Father Autry said.

We reached a clearing in the forest, and my father steered us to a *kadam* tree. It had a large crotch formed by three limbs spreading at about twenty feet above the ground. My father stood up in the stirrups and chopped several notches, for my teacher to stand in.

"Climb up into those footholds, Father-*sahib*, and set up your camera. Nandu, you stay with him, but go up to the next branch."

I swung up first, then helped my teacher with his camera. The other two elephants were sent to wait about two hundred feet apart at the edge of the jungle. My father steered Bhim Prashad behind a clump of trees. We were in position.

"If the leopard comes, Father-*sahib*, keep quiet and let the other two elephants drive it toward you until it is in range. Then take your pictures."

My father brought his hand to his mouth and made a wailing call, like an injured animal. The drongos and parakeets stopped their chatter. He waited and called again.

After the third call, Dilly raised his arm straight up. He had seen something. I heard the sound of someone sawing wood, and I knew right away it was a leopard. Then I saw movement. A large male was coming toward us.

One paw and then another, so carefully it stepped. We were up too high for the leopard to notice us.

My teacher began shaking so much that I worried he would fall out of the tree. I put my hand on his shoulder and pointed to the spot in the open grass where the leopard might stop.

My father wailed once more, and the cat closed in. In seconds he had reached the spot where I had said it would be, and Father Autry snapped away with his camera. "Nanda, this is so marvelous," he whispered.

The leopard heard him. It looked up and took a few steps, like he was coming after us.

"*Agat! Agat!*" shouted my father, and in a flash Bhim Prashad was charging toward the leopard. The frightened cat bolted into the forest.

"Lord have mercy!" exclaimed Father Autry. "That was the thrill of a lifetime. For a moment I thought he was going to join us in this tree." The whole way back Father Autry talked about the leopard and how he hoped his shaking hands had not made for blurry photos.

After we had all dismounted our elephants at the stable, my father said, "I am so glad you are pleased, Father-*sahib*."

Father Autry bowed. "It was one of the most memorable experiences of my life. Thank you, *Subba-sahib*."

I offered to walk Father Autry to the house near the warden's compound, where he would be staying. Father Autry's black clothes stood out against the red clay–colored road, even in the dusk.

"Nanda, how did the *Subba-sahib* lose his arm, if I may ask?"

"Father-*sahib*, please call me Nandu. It is my nickname and what everybody calls me at home."

"Why, of course. Nandu it is from now on."

"Now I will tell you. He was guiding a British lord, Lord Dunhill, a school friend of His Majesty the King, on a tiger hunt. The man was very stubborn. He refused to climb higher than ten feet above the ground to a safe shooting perch. *Subba-sahib* warned him that tigers can climb up to fifteen feet if they want to. He kept telling him, 'Your Grace, we must climb up several more branches to be safe,' but Lord Dunhill refused to listen. 'Tigers do not climb like leopards,' the lord said, and he refused to climb higher."

"After the episode with the leopard today, I would listen to everything *Subba-sahib* told me," Father Autry said.

I nodded.

"Besides the tiger, *Subba-sahib* knew there was also a tigress with young cubs nearby. He was worried she was hiding in the grass near their tree blind. *Subba-sahib* gave the signal to the other drivers to push the tiger out of the grass. The tigress came charging out instead. Before he could shoot, she leaped at Lord Dunhill and pulled him from the tree. *Subba-sahib* fought her off and saved the lord's life, but he lost his arm to the tigress."

"To risk your life for another—especially one that is disrespecting your superior knowledge—shows the depth of *Subba-sahib*'s character. It is not easy to live up to such a high standard as his charge, Nandu, but I know you can do it," Father Autry said, his eyes shining in the fading light.

I had never felt so proud of my father, and never so proud to be his son.

FOURTEEN

For most boys at my school, the forest at the edge of the playing fields meant nothing to them. They ventured into it only to fetch a flying soccer ball that strayed off the field. But I felt better just by looking at that forest. Sometimes I stared into it while the other boys played, its hundred tones of green and leaf shapes of all sizes fluttering in the breeze.

So when Father Autry proposed we explore it together, I jumped. "Come, Nandu, the best entrance for a hike is about a twenty-minute walk."

Twenty minutes was nothing for me, a boy from the Borderlands. On our way, we passed by the farmers' rice fields on the edge of the village.

"I am no stranger to paddies, Nandu. I grew up in Marked Tree, Arkansas, and that town also lay at the edge of rice fields. Even worlds that are very different can, in some respects, be incredibly similar."

"Do you miss America, Father-*sahib*?"

"I have lived in Nepal and India for more than thirty-five years, Nandu. This is my home. But I have returned to America many times to visit family and friends and to spend time at the Smithsonian Museum in Washington, DC. I have other work, Nandu, besides teaching. I collect samples for the Smithsonian so the world can better understand nature. I have made a life of studying birds and plants, especially ferns."

"You might want to think of moving to the Borderlands, Father-*sahib*," I said. "There is so much more to study here than in Gularia."

Father Autry smiled at me. "You may have something there."

When we reached the edge of the forest, he began reciting the names of each kind of plant we passed. I had never heard these names before. They were not English and nothing like Nepali. He told me that the names were in Latin, an ancient language, very little used except by biologists and priests. But every scientist anywhere in the world understands it.

"You know the Latin name of everything, Father-*sahib*—the trees, the birds, the mammals, the butterflies, even the toads. Isn't it hard to keep so many names in your head?"

"It is actually more difficult for me to remember what I had for breakfast, but that is part of growing old. Now look at this vine here, *Tinospora sinensis*. It is a member of the moonseed family. In America, our common moonseed is poisonous. The caterpillar of the fritillary butterfly that lays its eggs on the leaves eats the poison, and both the larva and the adult butterfly become toxic to birds."

"*Subba-sahib* uses this vine, too," I said. "We call it *gurjo*. Every part of it is useful. *Subba-sahib* has gout, some of the older elephant drivers, too. We boil the leaves to make a tea that treats the swelling. And the juice from the roots helps you vomit if you swallowed poison. It can also fight infection. It is big medicine."

"How do you know all this, Nandu?"

"*Subba-sahib* taught me."

At this point, our lesson reversed. Father Autry wanted to know all the plant names that I knew. So as we moved through the woods, I gave him the names in Nepali and Tharu and told him how we use the plant.

Father Autry paused and put down his rucksack beside a fern. He looked closer at the underside of it and let out a whoop. He then pulled out a little spade and began to dig. "How exciting!" he said.

"Let me help you, Father-*sahib*."

"Yes, but we must be very careful with the root. This might be a new species of spleenwort, and I need to collect the whole plant. I am very interested in spleenworts, Nandu, and western Nepal is thick with many types of them. I am sure of it."

We carefully placed the fern in a bag and then back in his rucksack. Father Autry was so pleased with his discovery, we decided to turn back. An hour later we had reached his quarters.

"Welcome to my bungalow, Nandu. Come right inside the dining room. We need refreshment after our expedition." Father-*sahib*'s cook had already laid out a pot of tea and cookies on the table.

"Nandu, do help yourself. Dahan Bahadur has just baked these," said Father Autry, as he poured me a cup of tea. "I assume you take your tea like most Nepalese, with half a cup of sugar?"

"Just three-quarters, sir," I said very seriously. I have no idea why it was, but Father Autry brought out my sense of humor like no one else I knew.

When we were done with our tea, he said, "Come, let me show you my pride and passion." We walked into Father Autry's study. "I had everything sent in boxes from Kathmandu. They arrived only last month."

The space was piled high with books and stacks of paper with fresh green plants sticking out of them. It was a small room, and so cramped it was hard to move around in it.

He reached for one of the green plants and opened up the covering sheet.

"Behold, Nandu. For me, the peak of evolution was reached before the age of dinosaurs. That is when the ferns of today began to appear. Many have changed little in one hundred and sixty-five million years. I wonder, how can nature improve on such an elegant design?"

"I did not know ferns were so old, Father-*sahib*."

"Ancient, ancient, and very diverse. There are probably twelve thousand species of ferns. Many species here in western Nepal are still undescribed by botanists. I would like to find them."

Father Autry was going on and on, and I chose not to interrupt this real scholar. So I waited and then raised my hand, like we were in his science class. "Father-*sahib*, what is a species?"

"Ah, yes, the very simple question, 'What is a species?' It has a very complicated answer, which I will explain to you in good time. But first come over here. I want to show you something else." On another table across from his stacks of dried ferns were bowls of sawdust and cotton balls and a strange sight—the skins of some birds.

"Oh, that's a red-breasted flycatcher, and here's a white-throated fantail. But, Father-*sahib*, why are they flattened so?"

"They are museum skins that I send back to the Smithsonian. I found these dead on the ground. A forest falcon might have dropped them. I am focusing for now on collecting the flycatchers of the Borderlands. I am impressed, Nandu, that you know their names."

"*Subba-sahib* taught me their names from the book an Englishman gave him. He also taught me their songs." I imitated the whistles of the white-throated fantail. "He is a bird of the riverbank forest, and you can find him singing on a woody vine we call *dudhi lohara*. He flies out and grabs an insect and then flies back. Flies out and flies back. And when he sings he spreads the feathers of his tail. I believe he is a very happy bird."

"My word, you do know things. Now, do you also know his scientific name?"

"We just call him *Punnkha Pucchare* in Nepali."

"His Latin name is *Rhipidura albicollis*." Father Autry paused. "Nandu, would you like to learn to be a field naturalist, one who knows the science behind what you see?"

"Yes, Father-*sahib*."

I had hardly thought about my fate since climbing the ridge with Dilly. But now it was clear that it was my destiny to be here at Future Scholars, to meet this teacher who held the knowledge of three men, maybe more, in his head.

FIFTEEN

A porcupine had been raiding the garbage pit behind the kitchen. The cook knew that I loved animals, so he called me when he was about to throw the vegetable scraps from dinner into the heap each night. Sure enough, within a few minutes, a family of porcupines came out of the jungle. Their long black-and-white quills rattled as they wobbled to the pit. They were soon joined by small civets and large civets, a long line of big eyes shining back at my flashlight. I would hardly call them wildlife, but they were all the wildlife Gularia had to offer—and it made me happy to see them.

It was nearly the end of April, the end of my first term at Future Scholars. I would have three months at home. Ever since starting to learn the Latin names of common plants and animals, I had dreamed of riding around the jungle on Devi Kali and practicing my skills as a naturalist.

The night before the start of summer break, I started packing a few things to take home.

Ballam was quiet, watching me.

"I will miss studying with you, Nandu. It is going to be a very boring summer." His father made him remain at school even during our holiday so that he would keep studying.

"Please come home to Thakurdwara at least once before school starts again. You must visit me at the elephant stable. We will go search for tigers!"

"Pray that my father will let me leave."

"I will ask *Subba-sahib* to talk with him. My father can reason with anyone."

The next morning, Dilly picked me up in the oxcart, and soon—our long conversation having made the time fly—we were turning onto the road to the elephant stable. I was feeling quite proud of myself for having made it through the first term at school, remembering how miserable I was at the beginning and how desperately I hated it.

Life can be interesting when you let it take you where it wants to take you.

My father stood up from the chair in front of Tulsi's hut when we pulled up. He wrapped his arm around me and held me a little bit longer than he usually did.

"I am so happy to be home, *Subba-sahib*," I said, looking up into his face. His eyes looking back at me said the same. "Everything looks just as it did before. Did the king change his mind?"

"I do not know, Nandu. The palace officials are not telling us much. Here, read this and see what you make of it, now that you are a scholar," he said winking at me.

I scanned the letter.

> To the Senior Officer-in-Charge
> of the Royal Elephant Stable,
> Thakurdwara, the Borderlands:
>
> We are taking your request under consideration. Until then, you will proceed with arrangements to prepare for the transfer of the stable in eight months' time.
>
> —The Honorable General K. S. Rana,
> Secretary to His Majesty

"Well, at least they read your letter." I sighed.

"Nandu, eight months is a long time. For now, no news is good news."

"Yes. Yes, it is!"

Although there was no news about the stable, my father did have a surprise for me. The night after I returned, we were sitting around the evening campfire with Ramji and Dilly, when he said, "Nandu, tomorrow morning before dawn you must saddle Devi Kali and take her up to the edge of Gobrela village. There is a grove of *mohwa* trees there, and they are in flower."

"Across the wooden bridge over the canal and to the right of the *kusum* tree?"

"Ha! One would think you had never spent five months away in Gularia. Exactly right, but you must get there before dawn or else the deer and the rhesus monkeys will eat up all the flowers that have fallen before you arrive. And by the way, I have invited the Father-*sahib* to go along with you. You have to pick him up first."

"Father Autry?" I asked. "Pick him up where?"

"Oh yes. That's right. I believe I forgot to tell you that Father Autry has decided to rent a little house here in the Borderlands." The yellow light from the campfire made my father's eyes dance.

"How did you keep such a secret?!"

"It was not easy for Father-*sahib* while you were at school. But he wanted it to be a surprise. He said it was you who gave him the idea to retire here."

I could not wait for the following day. "Will Dilly come with me? Or Ramji?"

"You are skilled enough that you do not need to go with another driver for this short trip," he replied, to my surprise. My dream of being a naturalist in my own jungle was coming true.

That evening, I readied Devi Kali's saddle. "Devi Kali, I am home for three months. And tomorrow we will be taking Father Autry with us to collect *mohwa* flowers," I told her. Devi Kali rumbled and tried to insert the tip of her trunk into my back pocket. I popped a *kuchi* into her open mouth.

I was tired from the trip home but too excited to sleep. I worried that if I closed my eyes, the sun would be up, and I would be too late to pick up Father Autry or find any flowers. So I grabbed my blanket and walked up to the dying fire and threw a log on. It was safer to stay awake until it was time to saddle my elephant.

I fell asleep briefly while listening to the *chunk! chunk! chunk!* of the nightjars. When I peeked at my watch, I saw that it was almost half-past three. I threw off my blanket and quickly untethered Devi Kali and fastened on her saddle. I tied a burlap sack to the saddle holding the containers for the *mohwa* flowers. At the last moment, I remembered to bring the walking stick my father had instructed me to take. He said that Father Autry might get tired, as he was getting old.

My teacher was already standing outside his bungalow waiting for us when we arrived.

"Good morning, Nandu!" he called.

"Good morning, Father-*sahib*!"

I gave Devi Kali her command, "*Beit!*" and she knelt down, first her hind legs, then her front pair. I slid off, my bare feet landing together on the cool night earth. The sun was not yet up to warm it.

I bowed at the waist and pressed my hands together at my chest. "*Namaste.*"

Father Autry also bowed to me.

As soon as we stood, I said slyly, "Father-*sahib*, should I ever have a secret that needed keeping, I would tell it to you."

Father Autry laughed. "It was difficult to keep it from you."

The sky had begun to lighten only by a whisper, but it reminded me we must leave quickly not to miss our chance at the blossoms.

I turned to Devi Kali and said, *"Pasar!"* She gently rolled to her side and stretched out her left hind leg to allow Father Autry to climb on more easily.

"Father-*sahib*, please hold on to this rope below the saddle while you climb aboard."

When Father Autry was seated on the elephant, I shouted, *"Sarbeit!"* and Devi Kali straightened herself. I rearranged the burlap sacks on the saddle, tied them off, and settled in front of Father Autry. *"Meil!"* I said, and she rose steadily to her feet.

The first rays of dawn filtered through the leaves. A red jungle fowl began crowing, and at last we arrived at the flowering *mohwa* trees. I tipped my head back and opened my mouth, my palms cupped in front of me, to catch as much of the drizzle of tiny flowers as possible. They tasted sweeter than the sweetest candy. I looked down and saw Devi Kali sweep the ground with her trunk, curling the tiny flowers up to her mouth.

Almost all the animals of the jungle love to eat the *mohwa* flowers. At night the fruit bats come to lap up the nectar from the tiny white blossoms. The flowers then fall to the ground by dawn the next morning.

Ramji told me that elephants love to eat them too, and if the flowers start to ferment, and they eat a lot of them, they sometimes get drunk and stagger around. I am not sure whether I believe him. But it is true that my father also uses the flowers to make the best *raksi* in the Borderlands.

I let Father Autry climb down first. His white wavy hair was sprinkled with blossoms. He looked up in wonder at the flower-laden branches.

"Did you try some, Father-*sahib*?" I asked.

"Oh yes, I will, but I enjoy watching them fall. It is a magic kind of rain."

As if Ban Devi herself had heard him, a gentle breeze blew through the grove, shaking down more and more blossoms in fluttering white sheets. I dropped Father's walking stick and quickly slid down, so I could use both hands to gather the delicate flowers. Father Autry helped, and we filled up our containers as Devi Kali stood guard from a few yards away.

Along the edge of the forest, the spotted deer and blue bulls were waiting for us to clear out so they could have their treat. By now the day was dawning and warming up the air. When I looked up, Father Autry had wandered up the dirt track. Behind him, I saw something bending over to pick up flowers from under another tree.

It was too dark to make out what it was. Suddenly, the animal stood up on its two hind legs and barreled on all fours down the path.

"Look out!" I shouted. I ran as fast as I could to catch up with

Father Autry, yelling and waving my arms in the air. I thought the sloth bear would retreat from my charge, but instead he huffed and snorted and kept coming straight toward us.

I heard Devi Kali's deep rumbling; she had covered the distance between Father Autry and me in a blink. She roared in anger at the bear and prepared to slap her trunk. The bear veered off into the forest. I took a long deep breath while Devi Kali trumpeted a last warning.

"*Raaa, raaa,*" I said, calming her and patting her trunk. "Father-*sahib*, are you all right?"

"My word! I didn't see or hear that bear coming. I am afraid he would have made short work of this old Jesuit. My dear boy, I am in your debt," he said, still shaking. "I had no idea there were sloth bears here. *Melursus ursinus*, now there is an unpredictable customer."

"Yes, we call them *bhalu*. Mr. Kipling in *The Jungle Book* made Bhalu nicer than he is in real life. *Subba-sahib* says that he will either run away or come straight for you."

"I must thank Devi Kali, too."

"Now you see for yourself, Father-*sahib*. She is the bravest, most intelligent elephant in the Borderlands."

"Yes, indeed." Devi Kali rumbled as Father Autry rubbed her trunk. "And she ran to protect you like a mother elephant would her calf."

I hid my smile and fastened the covers onto the baskets of flowers and lashed them to Devi Kali's saddle. Then Father and

I mounted, leaving the remaining flowers for the patient blue bulls and monkeys.

———

"Good morning, Nandu. I must say, this is another reward for making my home in the Borderlands: spontaneous visits from my best student."

I bowed and entered Father Autry's new bungalow. I had something serious on my mind, and I hoped he would listen to me. I prepared my words carefully in my head.

The dining room was cool and clean, and I recognized the white linen tablecloth and wooden Christian crucifix from his bungalow in Gularia. Father Autry showed me to a chair at the table and called out to Dahan Bahadur to bring another teacup and more biscuits.

We sat down, and when the cup arrived, he served me, pressing his finger into the china lid of his teapot, while he poured. He noticed the look on my face.

"What is amiss, Nandu? You seem upset."

"I still have one and a half more years at Future Scholars until I can return for good to Thakurdwara. And by then it might be too late. The stable might already be gone."

I went on to tell him the whole story of the stable being threatened with closure.

"I belong here, driving Devi Kali. But I have given my word

to *Subba-sahib*, and he has promised to make me a *mahout* if I pass my studies."

"Yes, I see your problem," he said. "And now I better understand how difficult it was for you to live in Gularia. Let me think for a moment, Nandu. Perhaps we can make your father a counteroffer."

Father Autry paused for a long time and then continued. "What if I offer to arrange with the school in Gularia to teach you here, in Thakurdwara? Would you be willing to help me collect specimens for the Smithsonian Museum after our tutoring sessions?"

"I would love to," I just about shouted. "Would you really be able to do that, Father-*sahib*?"

"Come, let us drink our tea, then pay a visit to your father. I must get his approval before I approach the headmaster of Future Scholars with our plan."

When we arrived back at the stable, my father had finished his day's work and was sitting in his favorite chair, a bottle of *raksi* in front of him.

He stood up to offer Father Autry a chair to join him. "Please, Father-*sahib*, sit here. Would you like to try?" he inquired, offering my teacher a glass. "The *mohwa* flowers make a strong but pleasant drink."

"Splendid. As a Jesuit and a naturalist I am eager to try it. Besides which, I nearly got into a tangle with a bear over it!"

My father poured out two glasses. The look of disappointment on my face made him reach for a third. "You may have a sip, Nandu. After all, it was your labor that provided the key ingredient." The men raised their glasses, and I joined them for a toast.

"*Subba-sahib*, besides young Nandu's bravery in the field, I am most impressed with his knowledge of the natural world. It is a gift."

My father nodded happily.

Father Autry went on. "Now I understand that he has three more semesters left to complete in Gularia. With your permission, I would like to make a proposal."

And with that, Father Autry laid out his offer, finishing with the part most of concern for my father. "I would make sure that Nandu would still receive the appropriate certificate from the school if he performs well."

"Your offer is quite generous, Father. But I cannot pay a full-time tutor of your stature. The school fees at Future Scholars are quickly using up my savings."

"I will not take anything for my service. It would be my pleasure to continue to teach my most avid pupil. Besides, Nandu has offered to help me complete my collection of flycatchers and other birds for the Smithsoniain Institution in Washington, DC."

My hands gripped the edge of my chair, while my father turned over the idea in his mind. "Thank you, Father-*sahib*. If the headmaster at Future Scholars agrees, I will be happy to have Nandu back at home. Let us go with your plan and toast to the education of Nanda Singh."

———

That evening, I walked Father Autry back to his bungalow. I always took my flashlight to light up the weeds that grew along the trail, looking out for kraits and cobras. Father Autry was already developing my Thakurdwara curriculum in his head. "We will start covering birds and plants tomorrow. And for our collection, let's focus first on the flycatchers and then move on to the robins. Also, can you get me slingshots? I might collect specimens on our excursions."

"I can get them at the bazaar. I know the man who makes the best ones."

"Good, then, I prefer them to a shotgun. I will have to find some BBs for the slingshots."

Without thinking, I nodded. "I can get those, too."

When we arrived at his bungalow, Father Autry motioned me inside. "Wait, I have something for you." Sitting on the desk in his study were several brand-new books. Father Autry handed me a copy of *Birds of Nepal* and *The Book of Indian Mammals*.

"Nandu, treat these like holy books, for that is what they are.

The creatures illustrated within are of a most exquisite design. God himself could not improve on their appearance."

I already knew most of the bird species found in the Borderlands. That night, I lit my kerosene lantern and looked through the mammal section. I had no idea our jungle held so many species of bats and rodents. I turned to the descriptions of the bears and started to read out loud about the species found in Nepal, the Himalayan brown bear and the Himalayan black bear.

I was looking for the shaggy black one with giant claws. There it was—*Melursus ursinus*—that is how Father Autry referred to it the other day under the *mohwa* trees. Before bed, I said a prayer to Ban Devi for *Melursus ursinus*, to wish him many ants and termites and all the *mohwa* flowers and comb honey he could eat.

SIXTEEN

My father never followed a calendar to know the time or the season. He would read the jungle for the cues he needed. "Nandu, in the hot season in early May, the black-headed oriole starts singing at six A.M. and stops at nine thirty on the dot." I would try to see the world as he did, using the sights and smells of the jungle as my guide and timekeeper.

But I also held tight to my new world of books. When I was out grazing Devi Kali in the fresh lemongrass, I would bring some with me to study. While most of the older drivers curled up on their burlap saddles for a late-morning nap, I stayed in my seat to read to Devi Kali, first from a book called *Among the Elephants* by a Mr. and Mrs. Douglas-Hamilton, and then from *The Jungle Book*. I would read and read, and Devi Kali would listen closely, sometimes bending back an ear when some part was really interesting.

Dilly loved to tease me, "Look, Nandu is reading to his elephant again." But I ignored him. No one but me truly understands that Devi Kali is my mother, that we are communicating in a way others cannot see or feel.

When we returned to the stable that day, my father told Dilly and me that we would need to go the next day to collect the last of my belongings at school. The first week of May was already hot in the Borderlands, so Dilly and I left before dawn on the only two bicycles owned by the stable. Soon we came upon Hala Ram Tharu, the thirteen-year-old son of the *Budghar* of Thakurdwara, and his uncle, Harka. They were also traveling to Gularia, each driving an oxcart filled with giant sacks of lentils and mustard seed to sell.

"Throw your bikes on top and hop in, *mahouts*. We are headed to market."

But the grain carts were moving too slowly for us. "Thanks for your offer, Hala Ram. We are going there, too. But we are in a hurry," said Dilly.

"Maybe we can join you on the way back, when you are empty!" I added as we pedaled past the plodding oxen.

After a few minutes, I turned to see Hala Ram and Harka far behind us. It was lucky I looked, because I could see three huge timber trucks approaching, creating a moving dust cloud. We pulled off the road to let them thunder by. They were headed east toward Nepalganj. "Who cut all those trees?" I asked Dilly. The logs were some of the biggest I had seen.

"You know what *Subba-sahib* says, Nandu. If you want to get rich, you become a forest officer in the Borderlands. You can make a fortune cutting timber and selling it in India. And you do not have to go far to smuggle it out. That footpath over there, or what is left of it, is the line." Dilly picked up a rock and with a short heave, tossed it across the border into India.

When we reached Gularia, the bazaar was already crowded with traders. In the distance, I saw three men, each more than six feet tall. Their long black hair was braided, and chunks of coral and turquoise hung from necklaces across their chests.

The three giants stared back at me.

"Nandu, they are Khambas, bandits and traders from Tibet. Don't stare back at them," said Dilly.

"Dilly, I look like them, don't I?" I said, ignoring his warning. My skin was the same color as theirs, and I was tall and long-limbed, like them. I had never before seen anyone, anywhere, who looked like they could be from my family.

I darted through the crowd, making my way over to the three giants. "Greetings, brothers, what brings you to the Gularia bazaar?"

They looked at me and laughed. One mumbled something in a language I could not follow, and the oldest of the three men spoke to me in broken Hindi. "We are traders from Kham. Go find your friend and buy some sweets, little brother." He tossed me a coin, and they all laughed again. I felt my skin tighten with anger and embarrassment. I left the coin where it had landed in the dirt.

I found Dilly standing by the sweet shop. The rich smell of dough cooking in butter carried across the food stalls of the bazaar. It was wonderful to smell sweets again and to see the brightly colored spices in piles like miniature mountains—the orange turmeric, the bronze ginger, the black peppercorns, ringed by hills of red, green, and yellow chilies.

Farther up the row of shops, the smell of burning rubbish overpowered the spices. In the stalls at the edge of the main bazaar, I found the one tended by a wrinkled trader called the Birdman. He was easy to spot; you only had to listen for the screeching of the caged parakeets, their green and blue and red plumage glinting inside their hanging cages.

Below the parakeets, the Birdman had arranged plumes of peacock feathers, deer antlers, porcupine quills, and pangolin skins. If you knew to ask, the Birdman would sell you the best slingshots in the district. He kept them hidden in a cloth bag, stashed out of view.

"What creatures are you mistreating now, old man?" I said as a greeting.

"Namaste, namaste," repeated a Talking Hill Myna in a cage above me.

"The bird greets me more respectfully than you do."

"I do not have much time, Birdman. I need several slingshots. And where can I find steel pellets?"

"Ah, taking up my trade, I see. If you bring me some hornbill beaks, like these here, I will pay you handsomely." The old man held up the bills of a great hornbill and an Indian pied hornbill. The Birdman sold the oil extract to local men who rubbed it into their scalps to treat baldness. It has no effect, but the Birdman convinces the farmers it can help.

"I am not interested in killing birds for you, Birdman. I will be collecting them for a great museum—the Smithsonian—in Washington, DC."

The Birdman whistled in admiration. "Then you will require my finest slingshots. Take these three. The handles are made from the *tejpat* tree, hard as ebony, yet still light enough. They will neither split nor splinter with age. And here are two boxes of pellets. Remember, collect any hornbills, and I will pay you handsomely."

I peeled off some twenty-rupee notes. A pied hornbill, its broad black wings clipped, perched on the cage holding the mynas. It looked so sad I wanted to buy him and release him into the jungle. "You are safer here," I whispered. "With your wings clipped, the jackals would catch you."

As I turned away to find Dilly, I heard the talking myna scratch out, "Stop! Thief!"

"You saw me pay, silly bird," I called over my shoulder.

Our last stop was the boarding school, where I collected my belongings and books. Ballam was so happy to see me, and I him, which made it even more difficult to tell him that I would not be returning.

"I will miss you, Nandu."

"I will miss you, too, Ballam. But remember, our friendship is not over."

"No," he said, "but now I will have to face the elephants' asses on my own again."

"I am not worried about you," I said. "You are tougher now."

"It is true," said Ballam, laughing.

———

That afternoon we made camp along the road on the edge of the forest outside Gularia. We had decided to wait until the next morning to hitch a ride with Hala Ram and his uncle. It turned out that the supplies for the stable, along with my books and belongings, were too heavy to haul back by bicycle anyway.

Dilly and I built a small fire and sat close to it, eating roasted peanuts and *samosas* we had bought earlier and four *jalebis*, two for each of us, which Dilly had purchased in the sweet shop. His eyes closed as he bit into one.

"Nothing in Thakurdwara tastes this good, Nandu. We are eating like traders."

After we finished, I showed Dilly the slingshots I had bought in the bazaar.

Dilly took one and felt the smooth handle. "Well, we had better get you practicing," he said, looking up with a grin. "We do not want to keep the Smithsonian Museum in Washington, U.S.A., waiting."

Soon we had set up a target, an empty can we tied high on a tree branch, and we began taking turns trying to hit it. Dilly was a good shot, and he showed me how to aim.

We competed until it was dark, and we could only separate the hits from the misses by the pinging sound of the rock against the metal can.

In the morning we were still groggy when two oxcarts rolled up to our camp just after dawn. Hala Ram jumped out to help us load our baskets and bicycles into his uncle Harka's empty cart. Dilly rode with Harka, while I went with Hala Ram.

"Did you sell all your lentils and mustard seed?" I asked.

"Yes, we did, Nandu," Hala Ram answered, "and at a good price. Now if we can reach Thakurdwara by nightfall, we will have a feast tomorrow."

A special occasion called for wild boar meat. The Tharu love to eat pork, especially the tender meat of the young ones. The villagers capture wild piglets from the jungle and fatten them in cribs.

"You and Dilly will be our guests. And you must bring *Subba-sahib* and Tulsi and Rita," Hala Ram added.

"Tomorrow is my birthday," I said, smiling. Or at least it was the day my father had settled on as my birthday, the day he found me in the forest. Perhaps they would let me bring Father Autry, too. I told him about my arrangement with my new tutor and the change in my schooling.

"How do you collect the birds for your teacher?"

"See?" I said, holding up a slingshot.

Hala Ram took the slingshot from me to examine it more closely.

"This is a good one, Nandu. Well-made."

"You may have it," I blurted suddenly. I was so grateful not to be riding my bicycle back to Thakurdwara and trying to balance all the packages. And Hala Ram had been so generous to invite us all to the feast.

Dilly decided to hop in the back of our empty cart. He was tired and wanted to take a nap. Soon he was snoring away as I watched the road home stretch out before me.

A few miles out of Gularia, the dense forest swallowed us up. The sun rose higher in the sky, and the drongos and barbets began singing. On the dirt track up ahead we saw a log across the road. A timber truck must have dropped it driving down the ravine.

A flock of jungle babblers stirred from the forest floor and began to chatter. Something was not right. I felt the hair stand up along the back of my head.

Uncle Harka urged the oxen around the log to the right. *"Tuk-tuk-tuk-tuk!"* he sang to his team.

"Dilly, wake up." I nudged him out of his sleep and handed him a slingshot. I motioned to Hala Ram to grab the bag of pellets.

"Get ready, Hala Ram," I whispered. "The jungle babblers are trying to tell us something."

Out of nowhere, three horsemen wearing maroon bandanas over their faces vaulted the log barrier and blocked our way.

"Give us your cash and gold," said one to Harka. "Give it now if you want to go home in one piece—"

Before he could finish his threat, I aimed a pellet that hit the bandit in the mouth. Blood seeped through the bandana, dripping down his neck.

The other two robbers raised their swords and were met with a hail of pellets from our slingshots. The robber with the dyed-red hair took one in his left eye, and it popped from the socket. He howled in pain, wheeled on his horse, and jumped over the log. The other two followed him, racing down the gulley and into the forest, back along the trail they had come.

I heard a whir in the air and a loud gasp of breath. A knife had struck Hala Ram. He slumped over, the blood soaking his shirt and flowing down his arm.

A Maroon circled behind our oxcart and raised another dagger to hurl at us as Dilly stood and fired. The pellet stung the Maroon's shoulder, and he dropped the blade. I fired again, and my steel pellet struck him above the nose. The robber turned his horse, and I fired a sharp rock that hit him on the side of his head. The Maroon slipped off his horse as it started to gallop away, and he landed with a thump on the ground.

Uncle Harka gently pulled the dagger from Hala Ram's shoulder, and I pressed my headscarf against the wound to stop the bleeding. "We have got to get him back to the doctor in Gularia," I said. "I know where the health post is." I pulled the cloth away, but the bleeding would not stop from the deep wound.

Dilly was on his knees next to the bandit. "Harka, Nandu, he is not breathing." Harka and Dilly and I all looked at one another for a moment, and then the world seemed to stop. We had knocked the wind out of the bandit. I had knocked him off his horse. He might be pretending. He might jump to his feet and grab another knife when we least expected it.

"We cannot wait. We must get Hala Ram to the health post. Let us bring this one to the police," Harka said. "Dilly, grab some rope. Bind his hands and feet for when he comes to."

"Why not leave him in the jungle?" asked Dilly. "The jackals will find him first. The police will only be trouble."

Uncle Harka had turned his oxcart around to head back to Gularia. "Make a bed for Hala Ram in the back," he instructed Dilly. "Next to the robber. And take his dagger."

And so we returned to Gularia, with me now driving the oxcart and Hala Ram sprawled out next to the man who tried to murder him. The robber's maroon bandana had slipped around his neck. His face looked frozen and vicious, not like the young Maroon whose face I had seen in Mohanpur.

I kept up a steady chatter the whole way back. Thirty minutes to go if the bullocks kept their pace. I apologized to them before slapping them across their rumps with the tamarisk switch. "*Tuk-tuk-tuk-tuk!* We are almost there, Hala Ram. The doctor will be waiting for us," I said.

Hala Ram did not whisper back. Just before Gularia, he shut his eyes.

PART III

A MAHOUT'S TRIALS

SEVENTEEN

The flat, one-story building that housed the Gularia health post was just ahead. The plaster was peeling from the front walls, and the painted metal signs bolted to the front were covered in rust. I worried about leaving Hala Ram in their hands, but we had no choice.

"Help! Help us!" I shouted to a nurse leaning against the wall.

We carried Hala Ram into the exam room, onto a cot covered by a white sheet, while another nurse raced out the door to fetch the doctor. No one noticed the bandit in the back of the cart, because I had thrown a tarp over him. He could wait his turn.

I held Hala Ram's hand, until the nurse gently pulled me away and closed the curtain.

"Can you save him?" I asked, facing the blank curtain.

But no one on the other side answered me.

Harka decided that it was best if we split up. "I will wait with

Hala Ram for now. Dilly, you ride your bike to Thakurdwara and tell the *Budghar* to come right away. Nandu, go to the police and file a report before someone spots the body in our cart. As soon as I know something about Hala Ram, I will join you."

I drove the oxcart to the police station and stopped in front. The guard sat on the front stoop, spitting out red streaks of betel leaf juice into the dust.

"We have plenty of straw for the jail, little brother. Keep moving," the guard said, waving me off.

Part of me did want to keep moving. I hesitated, trying to find the courage to speak.

"I told you to move on," the guard said.

"Come, have a look," I said to the guard, nodding my head toward the back of the oxcart. The policeman stood up, suddenly focusing on my bloody shirt.

I threw off the tarp to reveal the body of the Maroon.

"What is this? Is he dead?" he asked.

"The Maroons attacked us. There were three others, but they got away. We defended ourselves as best we could. He wounded my friend, who is at the clinic now, fighting for his life. I must go to him and his uncle. They are waiting for me. Can you please take him, sir, and put him in jail for when he comes to?"

"Certainly, just come in here for a moment and repeat what you told me to the sergeant."

The guard guided me through the police post and out the

back to a small building next door. It had only one window with bars in it.

"Sergeant, we have an incident to report," he called out. "Come this way, young man."

I entered the dark jail and was preparing in my mind what I would say to the sergeant, when suddenly, the guard shoved me farther into the cell and slammed the door behind me.

"Let me out!" I shouted. "I did nothing wrong. My friend needs me. Let me out!"

"You will wait for my sergeant's return," he said gruffly, and with that, he walked off and left me.

I squatted on the floor and took in my situation. In one corner was a jug of water. In another, was a hole in the concrete floor. The cell stank of old urine and what remained in the latrine. I told myself to stay calm. When the guard's superior arrived, I would tell my story and be released.

I heard keys fumbling in the cell door. The door swung wide open and the sergeant came staggering into my cell smelling of *raksi*. The guard followed him and began babbling about the dead man in the oxcart. Outside my window, the bullocks were bellowing, having gone without food and water for most of the day.

The sergeant shoved his angry red face toward me. "Stand up. What is your name? Where do you come from?"

"Nanda Singh, sir. I am a driver at the king's elephant stable in Thakurdwara . . . but, but . . ."

"A Tibetan driving an elephant? Ha, that is a good one." He pressed closer.

"How did you get so much blood on your shirt?" he shouted.

"I-I tried to stop the bleeding with it!"

"I see a dead man in an oxcart you are driving, and the bloody shirt you are wearing. How do I know you are not the culprit? Do you have any witnesses?"

"They are at the health post now. Go ask them!"

But before I could say another word in my own defense, the sergeant slurred, "Nanda Singh, I charge you with the murder of this poor fellow in the oxcart."

The sergeant staggered to keep his balance, then turned away and marched out. The guard followed him and bolted the door.

I was left sitting alone in the dark.

I wished Harka had listened to Dilly. We should have dragged that robber into the jungle and left him for the jackals.

***

The sun was beginning to set, and so were my spirits. It looked like no one was going to come for me. I would spend the night in a jail, with only crickets chirping in the drain to comfort me. I started to shake and could not stop myself. I tried to jump up and grab on to the bars in the small window, but I was too exhausted to reach them. There was no way I could squeeze through, even if I could work loose the bars.

The whirring sound of a bat's wings flitted by the window. I called to it, but it moved on. I could not believe I would spend my birthday, alone, in jail, charged as a murderer. If I had killed that Maroon, who would not believe it was in self-defense?

Someone would come for me, I told myself over and over. Tomorrow Harka would come with the doctor and explain everything to the sergeant. And in the morning the sergeant would be sober, and I could reason with him.

I tried lying down on the straw, but the first bedbug bites had me off it in a hurry. I tried lying down on the floor in different places, but every time I did, I felt roaches scurrying over me. So I moved to the corner, staring up through the barred window. I started imagining Devi Kali pushing through the wall, helping me escape this cell.

As the night set in, dark thoughts began to fill my mind.

I am only twelve years old, and I have already killed a man. What have I done? Why did I aim for his head?

"No, no, no," I said out loud, like I was arguing with myself. The words hung in the air. I tried to steer my thoughts: *Think of Devi Kali. Think of the jungle. Do not think of the Maroon.*

I eventually fell asleep on the hard jail floor. When I awoke, it was pitch-black outside, not a shred of moonlight was visible. Even the stars looked smaller, like they were shrinking away from me—afraid of my fate.

Shafts of light streamed through the barred window. I awoke an hour before dawn waiting for the day to come. But I had longer to wait. Midmorning the guard pushed a plate of rice under the slot in the door without a word.

Outside the temperature was climbing. There were no trees to shade my concrete cell, and it was already like an oven. I stripped to my shorts and waited, sipping water, in case they refused to give me more. I spent the day in solitude, my thoughts racing.

What have I done? Why did I not aim for his shoulder, like Dilly?

I started to get so angry I began pounding on the door. "Let me out!" I shouted. And then I remembered the attack on Mohanpur. I pounded with my fists and shouted even louder. "What kind of world is it that the Maroons are free, and I am in a jail?" But no one heard me. No one even came to the door to tell me to stop. I sank to my knees and sat there in a heap.

So began the longest day of my life, broken only by the guard removing my plate and handing me another at dinner.

The next day was no different from the one before. I tried to stay positive, thinking of the stable, of Devi Kali, and wondering where my father was.

By the third day, I had really begun to worry. Had anything happened to Dilly on the way back? Where was Harka? The guard would not answer my pleas for news about Hala Ram or anyone. He pushed the plate of rice under the door opening and pulled it back out, pushed and pulled.

I could no longer argue with my own thoughts. I began

hearing things. The heavy breathing of elephants and their rumbles, birds whispering to me. Then in the heat of midday the cicadas high up in the trees around the jail began their ear-piercing racket. This must be how you start to go crazy, I thought. I tried to stay focused and calm. Someone would come for me.

I thought about starting a hunger strike. I pushed the uneaten clump of rice back out the slot under the barred door. I would not eat. At least I would have control over that.

Please get me out of here. Someone.

It must have been near midnight when the deep *bu-ku, bu-ku* of a forest owl awakened me, and I had no luck getting back to sleep. I started pacing in a square around the cell.

Some hours later I heard a vehicle approaching. The whining pitch of the engine grew louder and louder until I heard its tires turn on the gravel road. It pulled up to the police post and stopped. Its headlights lit up the trees in front of the jail.

"Nandu!" a familiar voice called.

It was my father!

I shouted, jumping up and down, "I am in here!" but the barred window faced the back of the jail and the walls were too thick for anyone to hear my voice.

Then I heard something stirring outside.

A voice whispered, "Psst, Nandu."

A head appeared in the window, but I could not make out the face. I jumped, grabbed the bars, and pulled myself up to the window ledge.

"Ballam!"

"Do not worry, Nandu. Father Autry and *Subba-sahib* will get you out of here. Tomorrow some important people will come from Kathmandu."

"How do you know this, Ballam?"

"Dilly is here. I am standing on his shoulders. He came to the school to find me. He told me what happened."

"Dilly, is it you?" I could not see down that far.

I recognized his grunt.

"How is Hala Ram? Do you know?"

"He will live. The doctor said Hala Ram lost a lot of blood, but he was very lucky. The knife came close to his heart."

A jungle owlet shrieked nearby, making us jump in fright.

"Nandu, we have to go back before the night guard returns from his break. Dilly says Father Autry is a very powerful man. He called to the capital to have your case heard. You will be riding Devi Kali again soon. Do not worry."

And then they were gone.

———

The sun was already high in the sky, and the cell was boiling hot. The birds had stopped singing in the heat, so I knew it must be around noon. There was a rustle of keys, then one turned the lock. The door flung open. The sergeant came in with the guard.

"You behave, little devil, or I will throw you back in here," the sergeant said, as the guard shackled my legs. "You are going to your trial. When it is time for you to speak, admit your crime before our visiting judge."

I stood in the room in front of the jail cell and watched through the window, until I was summoned. I could see Father Autry and my father stand up from their chairs. Several vehicles with Nepalese flags mounted on the front fenders entered the compound.

The sergeant and the prison guard grabbed me under my arms, carried me out, and sat me in a big wooden chair. My father looked over and let out a curse. He was glowering at the sergeant. Father Autry and his driver, Syam Lal, grabbed each side of him, in case they needed to restrain him.

I heard Father Autry say, "Come, *Subba-sahib*, let us greet our guests. Your son will be with you shortly. Bear with this all for a few more minutes."

Out of the first car stepped a man dressed in a black hat with a black jacket over a white tunic and leggings, the uniform of a government official. He approached Father Autry. Behind him emerged several other officers in separate cars. In the last car was Watermelon Belly, the forest conservator-*sahib*.

A junior officer traveling with the group announced, "All rise in honor of the Chief Justice of Nepal Prithivi Narayan Dhakal."

The chief justice approached my tutor and then, to the great surprise of everyone, bowed deeply in front of Father Autry. The dignitary picked up the hem of my tutor's sport coat, and touched it to his forehead.

When he had stood, he said, "Dear Father, it is a pleasure to see you again, even in this unfortunate situation. Allow me to introduce you to the governor of the Borderlands, Jamuna Singh Mishra. And this officer in the red beret is the chief of the national police force, Inspector General Hari Lal Gurung. He accompanied me this morning on the flight from Kathmandu. You already know the forest conservator, I believe. Gentlemen, this is my esteemed teacher from St. Xavier's School, Father Robert Autry."

The governor gave Father Autry the *namaste* gesture and Chief Gurung saluted.

"Now, who is in charge here?" the chief justice asked, turning to the police sergeant.

"I am, respected sir."

"Sergeant-*sahib*, please explain why you threw this young man in your jail."

The sergeant told his story and explained the evidence against me. "Sir, the victim may have been a robber, but we cannot be sure. And the boy confessed to shooting him with his slingshot."

"Tell me, Sergeant-*sahib*, did you find any weapons on the dead man?"

"Two daggers, respected sir, hidden in his vest."

"Was there any blood on them?"

"No, respected sir, but there was another knife found in the oxcart coated with blood and the boy's shirt was smeared with blood."

"Inspector General, we will need to have the blood on the blade and the residue on the shirt taken back with us to Nepalganj and tested. My hunch is that the blood is that of the poor young boy, Hala Ram, who was struck by the knife thrown by the robber."

The chief justice turned back to the sergeant.

"Now, Sergeant, is there any other evidence of interest before we examine the body? Anything unusual that might give us a clue about how to identify this man?" asked the chief justice.

The sergeant did not reply at once. He looked at the guard before speaking.

"I repeat, sir, did you gather any other evidence or insights about this man in your methodical investigation?"

"He had a maroon bandana tied around his neck, respected sir."

The governor of the Borderlands whispered into the ear of the chief justice and the inspector general. Then they went over to inspect the body of the Maroon.

When they came back, the inspector general stepped forward. "You know who the Maroons are, don't you, sir? Now if we are to believe your view of the events, Sergeant, Mr. Nanda

Singh must have killed the robber in a premeditated manner, or knocked him out with his slingshot, bound him with rope, and cracked his skull.

"There is just one problem with this story. How do you explain the boy lying in the hospital with a stab wound that looks like it was made by one of these daggers? Do you suppose he stabbed himself to cover up for his friend? To make it seem more like self-defense than premeditated murder? And we have the sworn statements from Mr. Harka, Dil Bahadur, and Hala Ram, the boy in the hospital, who we have since interrogated, that they were ambushed by the Maroons and acted in self-defense."

The sergeant kept his face down.

"Sergeant, release the young man."

"Yes, respected sir."

I heard the words but they did not sink in. My mind was swimming. The sun was beating down, bright and hot, and I had drunk no water all morning. I watched as the guard removed the shackles around my ankles, and I heard him curse me under his breath. It was only when he finished and stepped away that I looked up and saw my father limping as fast as he could toward me.

It was suddenly clear. I was free.

"I came as soon as we heard what happened," my father whispered in my ear. "You have been very brave, *mahout*."

That word "*mahout*," was the only word I could hear. My father had never called me that—and never would—unless it was true that I was to become an elephant driver.

EIGHTEEN

"Now, gentlemen and Mr. Nanda Singh," the dignitary said, "I am afraid my plane is waiting. An officer from the Nepalganj unit will remain at the health post and guard it in case there is a new episode. Good day to you, Father, it is always a pleasure to see you. Good day to you, *Subba-sahib*."

Then Father Autry whispered something to the dignitary.

"Most important of all," he added, "I wish you a happy birthday, young man."

I bowed deeply to the dignitary, and for the first time in my life I did not feel like just a boy anymore. It was not because the dignitary had called me a young man, or because my father had called me *mahout*.

Something changed in me over the past three days in jail. I could not name it, but it seemed like each day in prison was like a year of my life passing by.

That feeling stayed with me while we visited Hala Ram at

the health post. Harka and the *Budghar* were by his side. They said nothing to me, but their faces showed how grateful they were.

Father Autry insisted that my father and I ride home with him in his Land Rover. As Syam Lal turned on to the Gularia Road, headed for Thakurdwara, a brilliant sunset erupted in the sky, reds and purples deeper than I had ever seen before.

I was sitting up front between Syam Lal and my father. My father placed his arm around my shoulders, and I leaned my tired head against his chest. The smell from my jail cell, and my isolation, still clung to me like it would never be removed.

All I wanted was to be back home. I had not slept much in the past three days and I could barely keep my eyes open.

I felt the vehicle slowing down and opened my eyes. Syam Lal had spotted someone up ahead in the headlights. We were still too far away to see clearly, but the man was waving to us. When the car approached, we could see he wore the beard and long hair of a *sadhu*, a holy man, who was dressed in a saffron robe. He was gesturing as if he wanted a ride, but Father Autry instructed Syam Lal to drive on. "Not worth the risk after what we have been through. This could be a trap." The Land Rover rolled along, covering the bystander in our dust.

When we reached the stable it was already dark. I walked over to my mother and whispered in her ear, "Devi Kali, I am home."

She heard me and rumbled deeply. I hugged her trunk and she lifted me off my feet, held me next to her chest. I was almost too tall for her to do this easily anymore.

"*Subba-sahib*, I do not know why, but we could not get Devi Kali to leave her tethering post," said Ramji. "She did not eat all day yesterday. I do not know how, but I think she knew Nandu was in trouble. Now that he is back safely we must hear the whole story."

"That will wait for tomorrow, Ramji. Now it is time for this young *mahout* to wash off the reek of that jail and go to bed."

I stripped to my shorts and crouched down while Dilly pumped cool water over me. While I lathered, he said, "Nandu, I am so sorry you spent so long in jail. It took two days for word to reach Kathmandu, and the police would not let us see you until we had permission."

"Those idiots." It was Rita. She held out some special shampoo. "In case there were lice. We don't want you to give them to Ritu or Rona." She was trying to make me laugh, but I could barely keep from sobbing. I pretended I had soap in my eyes.

"So *Subba-sahib* has finally made you a *mahout*," Dilly said. "We have to celebrate. Tomorrow let's take our elephants down to the river, and we will go fishing. Maybe this time we will catch something."

But I was not listening. He left to go back to the campfire while Rita stayed with me. Suddenly, my head and body grew so heavy I could not keep my legs under me. I collapsed on the ground, the weight of it all pulling me down at last.

Rita knelt next to me. She did not say a word but helped me back to my feet and back to my room. That night, slipping under the soft, fresh sheet felt so nice against my skin after the dirty hard floor of the jail cell. I fell asleep, a deep sleep, but later I awoke.

I felt my body being covered with a blanket. Then someone sat on the edge of the bed. A hand rested on my shoulder, my father's hand. I did not move. I was so tired.

I heard him whisper, "I am glad you are home, my son." He rose and walked slowly out the door, shutting it quietly behind him.

I pulled the blanket closer over my head to hide my tears. It was the very first time he had called me *son*.

NINETEEN

The verditer flycatcher flew to a higher branch and perched. I paused for a moment to admire its beautiful blue plumage in a fleck of sunlight and then let fly with my slingshot. The bird seemed to jump off its perch, but instead of taking flight, it came tumbling to the ground where I caught it in my hands.

Father Autry told me that collecting birds was how the world's two greatest naturalists, Mr. Darwin and Mr. Wallace, had begun their careers. If I wanted to be like them, I thought, I would have to start out like they did.

Besides, I had done so well that only a few species remained to be collected before Father Autry took them back to America. He would deliver them along with his fern collection to the Smithsonian Museum, then spend most of the monsoon season with his family.

"Thank you, Nandu. You are a great help. I will mention

your prowess as a collector to the curators at the Smithsonian."

I must remember to look up "prowess" in my dictionary, I thought.

The older drivers still were not talking to me much, so I spent more and more time with my tutor. I used to feel bad around them, but now I was angry, too. I had written a letter for *Subba-sahib* on behalf of our stable. I had defended our neighbors from robbery. Why could they not forgive me?

I found relief with my slingshot. I rarely missed anymore. A quick splash of blue and I spotted another verditer, with no stripe around its eye. It was the female. *Thwack!* In seconds, she had joined the male in my collecting bag. I liked the feeling of heft as it started to fill with my bird specimens. And then two spotted birds landed on the same perch—the young verditers. *Thwack! Thwack!* I had what I needed from them. On to the next species.

Father Autry taught me that most animals in the jungle do not die of old age but end up being killed by their predators. The old spotted deer killed by the tiger, the lame barking deer by the leopard, even the young grasshoppers by the shrike. I told myself that these verditer flycatchers probably only had a year to live anyway, before some snake climbed up and strangled them in their nest.

A trail of white feathers streaming through the riverbank forest set me in motion. Paradise flycatchers, the last species on my list. I started stalking them. The males flew to a cuplike nest where the female was sitting. Once I found several nests, it was easy. I staked them out and waited, like a tiger waits beside a stream where he knows the deer will come to drink. *Thwack! Thwack! Thwack!* I had a dozen filling my bag before lunchtime.

Hunting freed me from the stable, away from the cold stares of the drivers. I loved the sense of danger. On foot, alone, in the jungle. I had to keep my eyes open. Every stick is a snake, every shadow a lurking tiger. I did not tell anyone about my new hobby, not even Devi Kali.

I found Father Autry in his study, and he saw immediately that my collecting bag was full.

"I think I have all the species to complete your collection."

I opened the bag and removed the four verditer flycatchers. Father Autry gently picked up the male and sighed. Its powder-blue feathers gleamed in the light. "Evolution is an exquisite artist, Nandu, even if an unconscious one."

"Wait, Father-*sahib*, the most beautiful birds of all are still in hiding."

I removed the first of twelve Asian paradise flycatchers. *"Terpsiphone paradisi,"* I announced proudly. I thought I would impress Father Autry with my knowledge of the Latin name. I had spent so much time reading over the bird guide he had loaned me that I had memorized nearly all of the Latin names for birds from the Borderlands.

I took out one after the other from my bag. Several of the adults were all white with a black head and streaming white tail feathers almost two feet long. Several younger birds were a mix of white and brown. The four females were dull-colored but completed the collection of the species. I had been smoothing out the feathers when I heard Father Autry gasp for breath.

The expression on Father Autry's face reminded me of the sergeant in Gularia.

"Nanda Singh, what have you done? I did not ask you to bring me *twelve* of this species—or any at all. How unfortunate to have killed these marvelous birds. Some we simply do not collect."

I was struck dumb. I had committed a sin, but one that I did not fully understand.

I grabbed my bag and fled from the bungalow and headed for the banks of the Belgadi, where no one would find me. I climbed three steps into a small open-air hut along the river. It was empty. The only people to use it were old men, who sat under the thatched roof to pass time watching the river flow by.

He told me that all birds ended up dead somehow. *What difference did it make if I killed a paradise flycatcher or a common myna?*

It took some time before the answer floated by me, like a leaf on the river below. I was no longer a naturalist. What did the king call it when he almost shot Chuchi the tigress, a "crime against nature"? I reached for the slingshot, the same one I used on the Gularia Road against the Maroons, and flung it into the river.

"I am done with collecting birds. I am done with Father Autry." He was just like the old drivers. I do what is my duty, and everyone turns on me.

Why did I ever think I could trust him?

I was so angry that I barely noticed an older man coming down the trail. He wore his hair down to his waist, a long beard made red from henna dye, and a saffron-colored robe. I had seen him before.

The *sadhu* took one look at my face and said, "You seem quite agitated, my friend. May I sit alongside you up here in your riverfront palace, or do you prefer to be alone in your discomfort?" I moved my bag to the side to give the Baba a place to sit. I extended my hand to steady the *sadhu* as he climbed the stairs.

Now I remembered. This was the man we had passed in the Land Rover on the Gularia Road. He was the one who had tried to flag us down for a lift.

"My name is Nanda Singh, and I live at the Thakurwara elephant stable," I said.

The *sadhu* bowed his head. "I will listen if you wish to tell me why you are so sad."

I told my story, at least the part about collecting the fly-catchers. I had to share it with someone. Then I added, "Baba, I must tell you, I was in the jeep last month, there along the

Gularia Road. You signaled for a lift and we kept going. Forgive us for not stopping."

The *sadhu* waved his hand as if shooing away a mosquito. "It was better for me to walk to Thakurdwara and reach my new home on foot. A *sadhu* needs no chauffeur. Now what is the real source of your sadness?"

"I was proud to help my tutor, my friend, and now I have disappointed the one person who meant most to me besides my father and Devi Kali." I paused. "No, I feel the worst about shooting the paradise flycatchers," I confessed.

"They are indeed beautiful birds. When I was a child, we used to have them in our orchard. When the male flies with his long tail fluttering behind him, it reminds us that this life, too, can be an earthly paradise, full of wondrous things, if only we stop to look."

"Baba, I think my career as an animal collector is over."

The *sadhu* stared out at the river and spoke so softly I had to strain to hear him. "You cannot make this river flow back upstream, my friend. What is done is done. And it seems you do not know fully why the Father became so angry. He is a man of deep faith, and such men are hard to ponder. Perhaps there are hidden currents that you cannot see, as in this river. Our emotions are not always on the surface. You must look deeper for answers."

We looked on the river together in silence. Even when we

saw dark clouds gathering into thunderheads in the distance, readying for a burst of rain, we stayed under the thatched roof, letting the rain fall around us in heavy sheets.

⸻

As I rode Devi Kali back to the stable, I bent down and whispered near her ear. She raised it back to listen.

"I did a terrible thing. For the past two months, I have gone into the jungle alone and killed birds. No, I murdered birds. I am so ashamed of myself."

She rumbled back and lifted her trunk, touching the top of my head.

I rode her back from the jungle, stroking the tip of her trunk and her ears. I turned into the stable grounds and immediately saw the last thing I wanted to see at that moment: Father Autry's Land Rover. My *former* tutor was sitting under the gazebo with my father. Unfortunately, they saw me before I could turn away. My father called to me, gesturing for me to come sit with them. As slowly as I could, I got down and tethered Devi Kali.

I walked across camp and entered the gazebo. My father pointed to the chair where I was to sit, then he turned to leave. I started to protest, but he looked at me and made a "settle down" gesture with his hand. Then he winked to reassure me.

I could not look at Father Autry. I kept my eyes on his shoes.

Even after the rainstorm we had that morning, with mud everywhere, he wore his shoes. No one from the Borderlands would ruin their shoes this way.

Father Autry began to talk. "I regret my angry outburst. I know you meant no harm. You would never kill an animal unless it was to benefit science."

I still did not look up.

"You ran out so fast that I could not explain that my harsh words were triggered by an incident in my past. You see, when I was a child I shot a peregrine falcon, a bird much more rare and beautiful than that flycatcher, so that I could draw it at my leisure. I still shudder to think of it. The anger I aimed at you was really old anger at myself."

I still could not look up. Father Autry moved his black leather shoes back and forth.

"I am deeply sorry, Nandu. Can you find it in your heart to forgive me? I leave tomorrow morning for Kathmandu, and I will not be back until after the monsoon is over. I would hate to leave with hard feelings between us."

I looked straight into Father Autry's sparkling blue eyes. I was relieved, but I was sure I would never collect birds for the Smithsonian Museum again. "Of course I forgive you, Father-sahib. And I am so sorry I killed those birds. I am afraid I may not be able to continue my work in that regard. I will never kill another animal."

"I understand." I could see that Father Autry was much relieved, too.

We walked to his Land Rover, arm in arm, and I saw him off. He left for Kathmandu the next day, and I would not see him again until the beginning of September.

"Take good care of our jungle friends."

TWENTY

very afternoon near the end of May, thunderheads rose like
enormous pillows stacked one on top of the other, black and
gray and white. They promised rain, but then . . . nothing
fell, not a drop, only burning heat and humidity that made my
skin prickle under my sweat-soaked shirt.

I was out gathering firewood for the Baba. He had no family,
no one else to help him with his daily chores. When I had finished, I stacked the wood on Devi Kali's saddle. She also carried a
large log in her trunk, as if it were as light as a pencil, and off we
went to deliver our load to the *sadhu*.

I looked down on the dusty trail and saw the track of a tiger
leading to the temple. Devi Kali and I continued on to unload
the wood near the Baba's firepit. "Go and graze, Devi Kali, I will
be careful and call you if I need you." She looked at me and rumbled, like she was unhappy with my decision. I followed the tiger

tracks down to the stream that passes by the temple. The locals call it the Jogi Khola—the Holy Man's River.

I crawled along the riverbank and stopped when I saw them. Sitting in a side pool was a large male tiger, and upstream, only fifty feet away in another pool, was the Baba.

I moved on all fours back upstream. When I was opposite the Baba I motioned for him to get out quickly. But he only waved back and smiled at me. The giant tiger paid no attention to us. He only rolled on his side, settling in for a longer bath.

The Baba finally got out of the water and pointed to the temple. I met him there.

"Baba, that tiger could kill you with one bite," I whispered. "This temple is too dangerous for you to stay here."

"Thank you, my young friend, but when I go to my outhouse, I walk right by where the tiger rests. Even a holy man must poop once a day!" The sadhu cackled at his own joke. "The tiger and I have an understanding. It has been like this for a month now, ever since the weather became so hot. I believe this male has centered his territory around the temple and accepted me as a neighbor, one who means no harm. So I gladly share with him my sanctuary from the world.

"There is no hunting allowed near the temple," the Baba continued, "and he protects me from the robbers. Or so I hope."

I should have known that this holy man could make friends with a tiger. I vowed to learn more from him, whenever I could.

He had knowledge that not even my father or Father Autry had.

Avoiding the tiger, I returned home to graze Devi Kali near the stable, where the lemongrass was more to her liking. Rita saw us and came to visit, followed by her two feisty rhino calves, who chased each other around and played like children. Devi Kali took it all in, calm as ever.

Rita and I sat watching her graze. She ate slowly but carefully. First, she would twist her trunk around some stalks of lemongrass and yank hard, pulling the roots and a dirt clump right out of the ground. Each time, the broken roots released a sweet perfume. She then took the tussock and whacked it several times against her outstretched foreleg to shake off the dirt, before putting the citron-smelling grass in her mouth.

"She is very clever how she feeds, Nandu," Rita said.

"Yes, but she is not eating enough," I told her.

I had heard Ramji tell my father that Devi Kali's teeth were wearing down. I knew that elephants have six sets of molars over their lifetime. When the last set wears away, they can no longer break up the grasses they eat. They then must slowly starve to death. I could not stand the thought of this happening to my Devi Kali.

Heavy clouds suddenly blocked out the sun. The weather we had long been waiting for was upon us.

"Nandu, I think we better make a run for home," Rita said.

"It's too late!" I shouted. Then, for the first time in my life, I felt icy pellets hit my bare skin like little daggers.

Devi Kali rumbled loudly, then trumpeted against the hailstorm. She reached out with her trunk and pushed me under her legs. She did the same with Rita. The rhino calves came running, too. There the four of us sat, huddled together under her big body, watching the ice pop and jump on the ground. The hail fell fast, quickly making a layer of ice on the grass.

Devi Kali swung her trunk back and forth, as if counting the minutes until it would end. Nearly as suddenly as it started, it stopped.

We crawled out from under Devi Kali. Rita said, "Nandu, I cannot believe Devi Kali let Ritu and Rona right under her belly. She is like a mother to all of us."

I smiled and agreed, but did not want to correct Rita. Devi Kali was not "like" a mother to me, she *was* my mother.

———

The hail started the summer monsoon. Endless cloudbursts drenched the Borderlands, washing away the heat, which would not return until the following April. The elephants always get frisky at the beginning of the rains; the cooler temperatures give them more energy, too, or perhaps it is because the jungle turns thick and green again, with plenty of wild sugar cane and other good things to eat.

My father likes to say that the monsoon gives the Borderlands a break from the rest of the world every year. And for a while, it is true; we are like an island. There is no way in, no way out.

The heavy rains filled the rivers, making them spill over their banks, flooding the low areas. The water kept rising, coming right up to the edge of the stable, causing several female rhinos to wait it out close to where we tether the elephants. At high water, every creature must find higher ground or risk being swept away.

When the rain stops, the river retreats back to within its banks. I walked Devi Kali down to the river's edge to watch the rushing current, which was still too fast even for her, our strongest swimmer, to cross. To the east, the drivers said the Babai River was a brown ribbon full of uprooted trees, floating like a fleet of boats. On our way back home, another cloudburst opened up, turning her skin dark and less lined. She looked like a younger elephant again.

I got up at dawn the next morning to start sweeping out the stable. I waved to Ramji, who was leading Devi Kali down to the river, like he did every morning so she could have a long drink. Dilly went with him riding Man Kali. I was wrapping *kuchis* when Dilly rushed into the courtyard.

"Nandu, come fast. It is Devi Kali."

"Run! Get *Subba-sahib*!" I shouted.

I raced ahead and reached the spot along the river where Ramji sat next to her. She had collapsed. Soon, the entire staff of the stable arrived to try to raise Devi Kali back on her feet.

"She was walking along the trail and suddenly dropped to

her knees and then sprawled to the ground," Ramji said, shaking his head.

I leaned over and whispered in her ear. Devi Kali emitted the lowest rumble I had ever heard from her.

Where was my father?

"Don't worry, Nandu," said Dilly, who had just come up. "*Subba-sahib* is on his way. Remember that time one of my mother's chickens was about to croak? *Subba-sahib* picked it up, blew air into its butt, and chanted. The hen recovered and laid eggs for five more years. He will save Devi Kali, just wait."

Dilly was trying to make me smile and stay calm, but I could barely breathe. I lay next to Devi Kali in the mud and whispered into her ear. But her ear did not move forward and back as it usually did. She had no energy to even flap an ear.

My father arrived with several of the drivers. He checked the elephant's pulse and put a finger up her trunk. And then he leaned his ear against her chest. She had stopped breathing.

"Please wake up, Devi Kali," I pleaded. But the life had left her big body. I threw my arms around her neck.

"She has passed on from this life," my father said quietly.

All I wanted in this world was to feel her trunk curl around me. But I would never feel that again. I pressed my face against her rough skin. I wanted to lie in this mud forever and never leave her side.

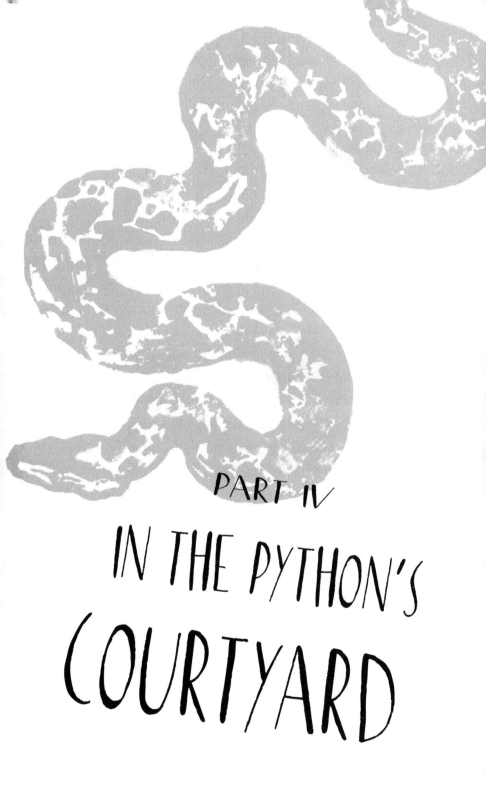

PART IV

IN THE PYTHON'S COURTYARD

TWENTY-ONE

Deep in the jungle, where no one would hear, I screamed at the goddess Ban Devi. "You did not have to take Devi Kali. You could have taken a crocodile, or a cobra. But you took my mother! I curse you, Ban Devi! What did I do to you?"

My heart ached so hard my chest hurt. My eyes felt dry from crying, and my throat was sore from screaming. I could barely swallow. My body was heavy and numb. It felt like the pain in my heart would never leave.

I spent mornings walking the flooded banks of the Belgadi. I walked barefoot, feeling the mud between my toes. I yelled into the roar of the river until I spent all my tears and had no energy left. There were leeches everywhere, and by the time I left the forest, they covered my feet. I invited the leeches to go ahead and suck the life out of me. It was mostly gone anyway.

Every day I could not wait for darkness, when I would climb

into my bunk, roll down the mosquito net, and seal myself off from the world.

In my dreams I would see Devi Kali collapsing in front of me. I wished I had been there when it happened. Maybe if I had been there, she would have had the strength to get back on her feet.

The worst nightmare was when I dreamed that I woke up, as if nothing had happened. I rushed out of bed to find Devi Kali tethered to her post, tossing bits of straw onto her head, waiting for me. But when I woke up for real, and ran from my cot to see if it was true, there was nothing to see. She was gone.

I have lost everything.

Those words were all that seemed to swirl through my mind. People tried to talk to me, and though I knew they were being kind, all I could do was look at them and silently say, *You do not understand, I have lost everything.*

I often stood alone by her grave. One day, the other elephants from the stable filed by, led by Bhim Prashad with my father guiding him. The elephants gathered close and touched the fresh dirt without any commands from their drivers. Bhim Prashad began a rumble and the other elephants picked up his chant. They missed her, too. It seemed like they were saying their final good-bye.

Weeks after Devi Kali died, I still could not lift my head up to look at the world around me. I no longer cared about being a naturalist. I could not imagine any kind of future. My father took me aside and told me an old story about elephants that had been handed down from ancient times.

"When a brave elephant like Devi Kali dies, a *muti*, a precious jewel, falls from its forehead. Nandu, you must look for it."

My father has special knowledge of the world beyond this world, so I believed him.

I went back to where Devi Kali had collapsed near the river and combed through the tall grass, but I could not find it. I searched near her tethering post and along the trail to the Belgadi River. Nothing. I only found more sadness everywhere I looked.

People tried to talk to me, but I kept my head down. At least, this way, I could explain to my father that I was looking down so that I might find the jewel. I stayed away even from Dilly and Rita. I only ventured out with my father, who took me with him to gather plants. It was all the human contact I could manage.

We found some black pepper vines heavy with ripe fruits. "Come, Nandu, let us gather these beauties before the fruit bats eat them all."

I pulled a few ripe clusters from the vines and stopped. I blurted out what had been weighing on my mind. "I think I am cursed. My parents disappeared when I was an infant. My elephant has died. What if you are next to leave me? You are a *jhankri*, who heals spirits. Can you lift this evil spell over me, before I lose you, too?"

My father turned to me, his eyes soft in a way I rarely saw. "Nandu, your only curse is your pain, which makes your whole life, right now, look like a string of wrongs. What you are feeling is grief. It is natural and will pass in time. Unfortunately, there is no chant to alter what naturally happens to us."

"But why could you save the chicken that died and not Devi Kali? I have seen you bring other animals, too, back from the brink of death."

"It was Devi Kali's time to die, my son. It was natural and right. Sometimes an event is out of sync with nature, only then can I alter it, to put it back in its rightful place. That was not the case for Devi Kali."

This was the second time that my father had called me his son. "Thank you, Father," I said. It was the first time I had ever called him anything but *Subba-sahib*. I had spoken softly, but I knew that he heard me, because he gripped his arm around me and squeezed me tight. For the first time since Devi Kali died, I felt some happiness. I had not lost everything after all.

I returned to her gravesite in the afternoon as I had done every day. We had buried Devi Kali under a large, old *mohwa* tree that would sprinkle her with tiny flowers next spring. In only a few weeks, a morning glory vine had already begun to grow, wandering across the bare dirt like a bright green trail to somewhere. By the next monsoon, the dirt would be covered by green growth. I sat on my heels and lowered my head. Suddenly, the heaviness returned.

Maybe my father was wrong. Maybe I was cursed.

"Talk to her, Nandu."

I jumped to my feet and turned around. It was Rita. She must have followed me. I turned back to Devi Kali's grave.

"I used to talk to her all the time," I mumbled.

"Then talk to her now. I was only four when my father died, but Dilly says I talked to him every day. Nandu, she is still watching over you. Here, I brought some lemongrass for you to give her."

"That was her favorite."

"I know. Put it over her. She will take it when you are gone. And she will graze with her ancestors. She is not alone now. That is what my papa told me about where elephants go when they pass."

I took the lemongrass from Rita and lay it in a sun pattern on the dirt. Then I tried to speak.

"Dear Devi Kali. Now you are with your sisters and cousins and nephews. You can graze together and never be hungry again. You are in heaven and every animal will be kind to you. The horse flies will leave you alone, and the king cobra has put his fangs away. You are in the safest place."

I took a deep breath to steady my voice.

"But you are different from your relatives. You are more than an elephant. You were my mother. You have taught me strength and courage and how to love animals. I miss you and will think of you every day for the rest of my life."

Rita had already left, but I stood quietly for a long time, remembering the day that Rita and I watched Devi Kali eat the lemongrass. I had sensed then that she was not eating enough. She was old. She knew that she did not have that much time left. Maybe she chose to die when I would not be there to see her. Maybe she knew that it would be too awful for me to see.

"The loss of such a companion must feel like a stone on your heart."

Another visitor. This time it was the *sadhu*. Was it possible that Devi Kali was sending my friends to comfort me when she could not?

I realized in that moment that I had neglected bringing the Baba food and firewood for several weeks. It was terrible, but I had forgotten about him.

"I did not hear you approach, Baba," I said.

"Not only elephant drivers can walk softly through the jungle." He smiled. "May I sit with you, *mahout*?"

"Baba, I am a *mahout* no longer. Neither is Ramji. Our elephant is dead. It is the law of the stable." It was true. We were out of work without our elephant.

"You will become a *mahout* again one day of a great elephant, like Devi Kali. Of this I am sure."

"There will be no more elephants. The king has decided to close our stable and keep only one here in Thakurdwara and send the rest to Chitwan. Even if we could keep the stable, my father says that we cannot get by another year with the small stipend we receive from Kathmandu."

I returned my gaze to the bare dirt in front of me. "Baba, do you have a prayer to lift the curse on me? My father says I am not cursed, but I fear he is wrong."

"The world is not what you think it is, my friend. At least not from the view you have now," he said. "Remember how an elephant carries a log? If the log is small enough, although still too heavy for you and me to lift, it will place it between its trunk and mouth and carry it home. When it arrives by the fire pit, it knows to drop the log without being commanded to do so. But if it is so long and heavy—that even ten men cannot move it— then the *mahout* must rig a chain around the log and the elephant will drag it back to camp. That is how you are now, Nandu. You are pulling a great log. You will haul it for a while longer, but not forever. Someday, others will help you release the chain, and you will be set free."

Those words "set free" reminded me of my time in the Gularia jail. I felt now as I did during the three long nights alone in the small brick-walled cell, isolated and alone.

"Baba, do you remember when we passed you on the Gularia Road when you were walking to Thakurdwara and begged a ride? Three days before that, I killed a man."

I had not said those words out loud since that night in the jail. *I killed a man.*

The Baba held my gaze with his kind eyes, and it stopped my trembling. When I regained myself, I told him the whole story.

"Nandu, as the Baba sees it, you saved your friend's life three times over. First, you fought off robbers who might have killed you and your friends, then you stopped Hala Ram from bleeding to death, then you drove him to the health post. I would say that what you did in one day is more than what some men do in a lifetime."

"Thank you, Baba."

"Now, I will tell you a story. I have told it to no one, and by telling you in confidence, I place great trust that this story will be kept between us."

"I will hold your secret, Baba."

His face changed and almost clenched. "You are not the only one to have taken a life. I was a very wealthy man, but something happened once . . . and children died. It was my fault. I had failed to pay attention to what was happening in front of me."

He paused.

"So I stopped being that person. I began to practice a new daily ritual, I would pray and recite the holy texts. I was inspired by the story of the Buddha, so, like him, I left my home and lived in the forest for three years, to contemplate my way alone. I will not say more of this old life nor I hope will you."

I nodded in assurance.

His kind smile returned and he became the Baba again. "Of

course you will feel grief over what happened on the Gularia Road like I once felt. You will feel this for a long time and that is natural. But you must also feel that you gave life back to Hala Ram."

"How did you end up here at this temple in Thakurdwara, Baba?"

"On the Gularia Road, where you saw me, I met another *sadhu*, going in the opposite direction. He told me about a temple he had visited years before, outside Thakurdwara. He said it was only one room and next to it sat a small thatch hut inside a great jungle. He said he had heard the temple had not been tended in a long time.

"The morning I arrived, I noticed an enormous web in a corner, in which a spider had captured a tailorbird. The tiny creature struggled to free its tangled wings from the spider's silk. Before the giant spider could sink its fangs into the poor little thing, I quickly released the struggling bird. This time I did not hesitate, as I had done in the past.

"When to act on what you see and when to accept what you see around you? I do not know the answer to this question. What I do know, Nandu, is that you had the courage to act. What we do and what happens to us is the same thing. That is all I know about fate. One day, when your log of grief breaks free, you will see the good around you and in you. You are not cursed, my friend. You are blessed."

It was getting late, and I had to head back to the stable for evening chores. I thanked the *sadhu* for his wisdom and promised to continue to bring him firewood and food, when I could.

Halfway home, in the middle of the forest, I felt something following me. I turned and saw a *dhole*. He was alone. He stopped in his tracks and looked me in the eye. We spoke to each other without words. I know that sounds impossible, but it is true. And as I walked back home, I suddenly realized that the log that I was dragging had become lighter.

TWENTY-TWO

The day the wind starting blowing from the west, the heavy rain of the monsoon stopped, just as my father said it would. The riverbanks reemerged as though the plug on an enormous drain had been pulled. There were puddles and pockets of mud, but the roads were passable again. The whine of a familiar jeep approaching the stable broke the quiet of a peaceful day in the Borderlands. The forest conservator-*sahib* was here to check up on us.

The conversation did not last long. The conservator-*sahib* signaled for the driver to turn the motor off. But rather than get out of the jeep, Watermelon Belly spoke to my father through the rolled-down window. Rita and I were within earshot, playing with the rhino calves. I motioned for her to stop and listen. We had to strain to hear his words.

"You have three more months to be ready to march to Chitwan. India has threatened to stop selling elephants outside

177

the country, including to Nepal. We cannot count on any new purchases to make up the loss."

To lose Devi Kali was hard enough. To lose my home was too much. I hated to think what would happen to my father and me and the other drivers. I wondered if my father might turn to drink, as Ramji had done since Devi Kali died. Too many days by the campfire with nothing much to do, he broke a rule that my father as *Subba-sahib* would not bend.

"A driver may drink all he wants at night, but he must be sober during the day," my father told him. But Ramji did not listen, so my father had no choice but to relieve him of his duties. Because Ramji had been one of the stable's most trusted drivers, my father did not send him back to his village but arranged for Ramji's pension to begin and allowed him to remain in camp and help out with camp chores. But now he was an unemployed driver in a stable that was doomed to close. Where would Ramji go?

I jumped up, not waiting for the jeep to leave. Since I no longer had Devi Kali to care for, I had been helping Rita look after the rhino calves. They had grown so much, we had to stand to feed them—their backs were now above Rita's chest. It looked funny to see the big creatures still taking their warm milk from bottles. Rita and I called them the ancient babies who would never grow up. But we knew, of course, that they would, and someday we would have to let them join the wild rhinos in the jungle.

Rita was strangely silent. She was normally such a chatter-box I did not know what to make of it.

"Nandu, did you hear the forest conservator-*sahib* say that India would not sell any more elephants to Nepal? It gave me an idea. If I can raise rhino calves, why not raise baby elephants?"

I smiled. Her idea reminded me of a book I had brought home from the boarding school.

"Come with me, Rita. I have to show you something."

We ran to the barracks with the rhino calves chasing after us. I went into my room and pulled out the book about elephants in zoos in the U.S.A.

"Rita, elephants are three times more expensive for zoos in America to purchase from India than for us in Nepal, because the elephants must be transported over the sea. This book men-tioned a zoo in the city of Atlanta that decided to breed their own elephants. One male has already fathered seven calves, each from a different female. Here, look at this picture."

"We must tell *Subba-sahib*," Rita practically shouted at me.

My father was sitting by himself under the gazebo, drink-ing a cup of tea. At least I hoped it was tea, and not *raksi*. A visit from the forest conservator-*sahib* usually ended with my father drinking long into the night—something he rarely did other-wise. Ritu and Rona had followed Rita and me, and now flopped down at our feet like tired dogs.

"You have done well, Rita, with these young rhinos," my father said. "Your father would be proud to see you with them."

"Thank you, *Subba-sahib*, I do think I am a natural—" Rita paused, her eyes darting at me. She had lost her nerve.

"Rita has had an idea," I said. "One that could save our stable. You must hear her out."

"Go on, Rita, I am listening."

My father looked amused when Rita proposed raising elephant calves like the rhino calves she had raised. Then I showed him the pictures of the young elephants born and raised in Atlanta posing with the head trainer.

"You mean there are *Subba-sahibs* in American zoos?" he asked.

"Not exactly. They are not running a stable, but they are trying to keep a collection of elephants for people to see and for scientists to study. Excuse me, *Subba-sahib*, but we overheard the forest conservator-*sahib* say that we may not even be able to buy elephants anymore from India. Now we have the same problem the American zookeepers do."

"But, Nandu—"

"All of our domesticated elephants come from India, so what will we do in ten years when the older elephants here and at the Chitwan stable start to die?"

Rita nodded. She was fidgeting so much I thought she would fall down.

"But, Nandu and Rita—"

That was her cue. "*Subba-sahib*, what if we turned our stable into an elephant breeding center? Then we would supply

Chitwan with young elephants for the king's hunt," she said.

"Rita and Nandu, I think this is a fine idea."

I knew that tone. He wanted to encourage us, without telling us what he really thought—that our idea was hopeless.

"Please, *Subba-sahib*," I said, "you must at least consider presenting this idea to your friend at the royal court. If Rita can raise two rhino calves on her own, we drivers and Rita could raise baby elephants and train them when they grow up. They would be the finest, most well-cared-for elephants in the world."

My father looked at both Rita and me. "I have no doubt. This is a good idea. There is only one problem, as I see it, but it is a big one. Bhim Prashad and Mahendra Gajh are past their prime. We have no tusker here at our stable young enough to breed our females."

"Then we will think of a way to find one," I said.

My father stood, threw what was left in his drink onto the ground, and tapped the empty cup on his head. "We will all put our heads together."

As we watched my father walk away, Rita did not say anything. Then suddenly she turned and hugged me hard.

"I cannot breathe," I said, faking it a little.

She hugged me harder.

For the first time in a long time, I began to smile.

At last, Father Autry returned from his summer in America. It was only three months, but it seemed like he had been gone for years. We walked together to find my father in the stable.

"I missed you, Nandu," he said. "And the Borderlands, of course."

"I missed you, too, Father-*sahib*. I . . . I have to tell you something," I said, my voice starting to waver. "While you were away . . ." I could not finish the sentence. My sadness had lessened greatly, but then sometimes it could return in full, in an instant.

"I heard the very sad news about Devi Kali. I am so sorry, Nandu. And I know you are now worried about losing your stable."

"Yes, but I have some good news, too," I said, trying to brighten. Rita approached with the calves to greet Father Autry. She gave him the *namaste* gesture, and he bowed back.

Then we told him about her idea to start a breeding center here in Thakurdwara. Father Autry's eyes lit up when I told him we had taken the idea partly from a book from the Future Scholar's library.

"This is a very clever idea—a breeding center. Tomorrow you must work out the arithmetic with your father's help. He will need to list for you the age of all the female elephants in Nepal and determine which are past breeding age. If you can make a strong case for the herd diminishing, the king might listen favorably to your proposal."

When Father Autry left to settle back into his bungalow, Rita and I started our calculations using our females here at the stable. When Rita and Dilly's father was alive, a female in our stable might be let out to breed with a wild male if it was her time and there was a need for a new calf. That is how Devi Kali gave birth to several calves.

But it is a dangerous business: if the female does not like the wild male and he keeps trying to breed her, he can injure her severely. And once, a wild male charged through camp and nearly killed several drivers trying to fight him off. Our plan was safer.

There was a lot of information to go through in my father's files. But what we found shocked us all. The king has one hundred and thirty elephants at three different stables. But there are only two males of breeding age. They are both at the small stable near Birgunj and mostly used for ceremonies in Kathmandu.

Of all the females, more than half were already too old to breed. If we did not start now, in twenty years the stables would be filled with many old elephants.

Rita and I showed our figures to my father, who suggested we go at once to tell Father Autry. I let Rita run ahead of me, walking carefully behind. I was holding the papers and did not want them to blow away. Her long black hair flying back on the breeze made me think about us as children, racing down the road, only half the size we now were.

At the bungalow, Father Autry was sitting outside in a chair with his eyes covered by binoculars. When he saw us, he pretended to refocus the binoculars on us.

"A very strange species indeed," he said.

But we had no time for jokes. We handed him our work, both talking at once. He immediately went inside to retrieve his glasses so he could read it.

"Rita and Nandu, you have made a sound case. I will be happy to help in any way I can."

Rita made the *namaste* gesture as if she was about to leave. "Before you go, I have been meaning to ask, Rita, if you might like to join Nandu and continue your studies?"

"Oh yes, Father-*sahib*!" Rita cried.

Father-*sahib* turned to me with raised eyebrows to assess my reaction. I shrugged, pretending not to care, when the truth was—to my own surprise—I liked the idea very much.

TWENTY-THREE

My father and I were at the burial ceremony of an old Tharu from Thakurdwara. The site was not far from where Devi Kali was laid to rest. "We Tharu bury our dead, Nandu, with the head pointing south. That way, the first thing the soul sees when it rises is the Himalayas, and the person is blessed and goes to heaven."

We had buried Devi Kali in the same direction, and now I imagined her rising up, grazing in endless fields of lemongrass. I so missed her.

"Good day, *Subba-sahib* and Nandu." It was Syam Lal, Father Autry's driver, waving to us. "Have you taken your rice?"

"We have, thank Ban Devi. What brings you over to us?" my father asked.

"The Father-*sahib* and another gentleman are waiting at his bungalow, *Subba-sahib*. They would like to talk with you, if you are free for tea and cakes."

"I am afraid I have little time today," said my father, shaking a letter in his hand to indicate the reason. "Please convey my apologies." The letter he had just received was from the palace, and though he had not spoken about it yet, the news did not seem good.

"Please forgive my persistence, *Subba-sahib*, but Father Autry and his visitor have an urgent matter to discuss. He was most insistent."

"Very well," my father said, folding the letter against his thigh and putting it in his pocket.

"And Nandu and Rita are to come, too," said Syam Lal.

When my father, Rita, and I entered the bungalow gate, we found Father Autry sitting on the front porch, waiting for us. Sitting next to him was the Baba.

"Ah, *Subba-sahib*, Rita, and Nandu, welcome, welcome. We were just discussing some passages in the Upanishads. Please, we are about to have tea and some special cakes. For today is an auspicious day."

I looked at Rita. My stomach got very tight, so I tried to relax it by taking a deep breath, as my father had taught me.

"Dahan Bahadur, please serve the cinnamon-raisin cakes that Nandu likes so much and pour tea for our honored guests."

The Baba smiled, but my father did not. Father Autry immediately sensed something was wrong.

"*Subba-sahib*, I think you have some news that is perhaps not so cheerful. Has something happened?"

"The day has not moved in such a welcome direction for our stable." My father took the letter from his pocket and handed it to Father Autry. I read over his shoulder, and for once, my father let me.

To the Senior Officer-in-Charge
of the Royal Elephant Stable,
Thakurdwara, the Borderlands:

We have considered your request and at the advice of
the royal trackers and the forest conservator for the
Borderlands, we will proceed as planned to shift all
future royal hunts to Chitwan. Be advised that the
forest conservator will take charge of the elephants in
December and march them to Chitwan. His Majesty
thanks you warmly for your service over the past three
decades.

—The Honorable General K. S. Rana,
Secretary to His Majesty

"Well, it does seem dire," Father Autry said, after reading it. He placed the letter on the table in front of the Baba, who would not touch it.

"But the plan for a breeding center appears quite sound. I have explained it to the Baba, who agrees. There is only one major problem as the Baba and I see it, if I may speak for the two of us?"

The Baba bowed his head and gestured for him to continue.

"You need to purchase a breeding tusker, and rather quickly, if I am correct," Father Autry continued as he poured the tea. "Please, try one of these orange cream biscuits."

As my father took a cookie, Father Autry reached under the tablecloth and pulled out a small leather satchel. He handed it to my father. "This should turn the day around, *Subba-sahib*. Please open it. The Baba wishes you to have it, and acting as his solicitor in the matter, I fully agree."

My father put down his biscuit and opened the satchel.

"What is this?" he asked.

"Sixty-five thousand rupees. There is your tusker, or at least the money for purchase."

"I cannot accept your offer, no matter how kind. We must find our own way out of this."

Father Autry paused and started a new tack. "*Subba-sahib*, I understand your position. The Baba wants to make this a business arrangement. The Baba needs a tusker for his ceremonies to Lord Ganesh. I am a silent partner in this agreement, and I am in need of a tusker for use in my natural history and collecting expeditions to be accompanied by my driver Nanda Singh. I cannot risk another attack by a sloth bear while on foot."

"But we have no money at the stable in our budget to either purchase or support a tusker, and the forest conservator-*sahib* knows it. He will ask hard questions," my father explained.

"We have thought of that, too. My small stipend will cover the upkeep. You may tell the conservator-*sahib* that this is our elephant on loan to you. So the co-owners, the two of us, require a purchase of a male. You may use him for breeding, but you must allow us occasional use. This way you will not be questioned as to where you found the money. Our only condition is that Nandu be assigned to this new elephant." The Baba nodded and Father Autry winked at me.

I looked at my father. He is a very proud man, but I think he realized there was no choice but to accept the gift.

"Let us discuss these terms," my father said.

Rita kicked me hard under the table, and I tried not to grimace.

While my father and Father Autry continued talking, the Baba excused himself and motioned for me to follow him into the other room.

"Baba," I whispered. "You have no money. You are a *sadhu*. How can you afford this?"

"Remember my secret story, Nandu."

"I told no one else, and I will join Devi Kali before I tell anyone," I reassured him.

"You recall that I was once a very rich man. Before I left my old life, I retained sixty-five thousand rupees in case of an emergency. I see clearly that my emergency has arrived. I was carrying the wad of bills in a hidden pocket of my vest. But it began to feel so heavy. Now I feel as if the last burden has been lifted from me."

"Thank you, Baba."

"Nandu, you must be off soon to find a great tusker, my dear young friend. The fate of the stable and our jungle family rests in your hands."

TWENTY-FOUR

ate keeps its own calendar, I guess. Only Ban Devi herself could have planned the timing of this gift. In just four days, the greatest elephant fair in all of India, the Sonepur *Mela*, would take place in the state of Bihar, two days travel from Thakurdwara. Elephants are marched there from all over—Assam in the east, Rajasthan in the west, and Kerala in the south.

There was bad luck, too. My father's gout was worse, and now he walked in pain. I had gathered *gurjo* vine leaves and boiled a handful for him to drink to help relieve his discomfort, though it did not seem to help. He was still lying on his cot at midday.

"Nandu, I must face the truth. I will not be able to travel to Sonepur," he said. "I used to travel to the *Mela* with Dilly's father, Bir Bahadur, to purchase elephants for the king's stable before you were born. He was the best judge of elephants I have ever known. Let us hope he passed down some of his wisdom to his son. Go fetch Dilly, and I will give you my instructions."

"Yes, *Subba-sahib*."

I ran across to the barracks and returned quickly with Dilly.

"Sit down, young drivers, we have important business to attend to. Dilly, do you remember anything that your father taught you about how to judge an elephant?"

Dilly swallowed hard and then spoke. "Never buy an animal with yellow eyes. Walk away from an elephant with a black tongue. Never pick one with a trunk too short or a tail too long. Always check the ears. An elephant with many ear folds will die before the next harvest. And, for a tusker, steer clear of long legs.'"

From the bright look on my father's face, Dilly had answered correctly.

"You two will go together to the Sonepur Elephant Fair. Dilly, you will select our tusker and do the bargaining. Nandu will count the money and write the bill of sale.

"There are as many cheats as honest dealers at Sonepur," he continued, "and you are sharper with figures and words than anyone in the stable, Nandu, far better than I."

"Yes, *Subba-sahib*, of course." I paused and thought some more. "But what about Phirta or Joker? Perhaps they would want to go in my place?" I was worried that the older drivers would resent me even more, the youngest driver in the stable being sent to purchase a tusker.

My father smiled. "Nandu, you are right to think about the reactions of other men. That is how a *Subba-sahib* thinks. You see, however, if I sent Phirta, he would take the money and drink it all up and run away. And Joker Ram knows how to train elephants, but he is half-blind. If I sent him, he might come back from Sonepur driving a camel."

Dilly and I laughed.

Then *Subba-sahib* became serious. "Now listen. Here is the satchel. In it is all we have—sixty-five thousand rupees. We need you to come back with a breeding tusker. I am counting on you."

Dilly never lacked confidence. "Do not worry, *Subba-sahib*. We will return from Sonepur with a tusker, who can breed all of our females."

My father raised his arm and signaled for me to help pull him up to standing. "You must leave soon. The *Mela* starts in four days and the best elephants will be bought quickly. But first, Nandu, Dilly, we must prepare you for this journey."

Dilly and I looked at each other but said nothing. I was so glad he was my friend, like an older brother. I could never have faced the journey to Sonepur alone. But with Dilly, I felt ready for anything fate had in store for us.

We followed my father as he hobbled down the trail to his special grove of trees by the river. He began a chant to Ban Devi, lit incense, and waved smoke over us. He dabbed our foreheads with rice and vermilion powder. As we left the grove, we walked between two water-filled vessels, set there for the ceremony.

We had his blessing, and we hoped Ban Devi's as well.

When he had finished, my father reached into his shirt pocket. "Give me your right hand, Nandu. I almost forgot the most important ceremony of all."

I held out my arm, and he slipped a bracelet over my wrist—an elephant hair bracelet. He closed his eyes and chanted again, performing another *jhankri* ritual. Then he looked deep into my eyes.

"Nandu, before she passed, I took some tail hairs from Devi Kali and gave them to Phirta to weave together. She was a courageous elephant. Wear this bracelet at all times, and she will protect you on your way."

I held the bracelet against my heart as Dilly and I set off on our journey.

Outside Thakurdwara, Rita caught up to us on her bicycle. "I am coming with you," she said.

"Rita, go back home and take care of your rhino calves. They need you." Dilly knew how to handle his sister.

Her face grew long. "Then take this, Nandu," she said, handing me a small purse. "It's my wages for caring for the ancient babies. Three hundred rupees. Put it to the price of a great tusker."

"Thank you, Rita. Soon you will have elephant babies to care for, too."

We took a shortcut through the forest to reach the towns by the edge of the Borderlands. We hoped to arrive at the village of Gobrechar by dark.

The sun was sinking over the ripening rice fields, when we finally saw Gobrechar in the distance, one of many in the Borderlands ruled over by a wealthy landlord named Lok Nath. The Tharu farmers gave him large shares of their crops as rent or to pay off their debts, which never seemed to grow smaller.

"They call Lok Nath the Python because he squeezes the savings out of all the people around him," Dilly said.

Just outside the village, a hill tribesmen, a Tamang like Dilly, spotted us running through the grazing lands at the edge of the jungle. Seeing we were of mountain stock, he shouted out to us in a Tamang dialect, "Do not run so fast, my friends. The sun is about to take its rest and so should you."

"We are in a hurry, *Shambo*," I replied.

"We must reach the Sonepur *Mela* by tomorrow night to buy an elephant," Dilly explained.

"What would mountain boys want with an elephant? Go buy yourself a yak, my young friends, the milk is far tastier." Pleased with himself, the old Tamang chuckled.

There is a story told by the Tamang that the first sound uttered by most newborn babies is a wail, but the Tamang infant lets out a giggle and goes on laughing until his dying day.

He continued, "No need to run all the way to Sonepur if it is the turds of an elephant you want to inspect. Take a look at the Python's tusker."

"Is he for sale?" I asked.

"You never know. The Python has no use for the male he bought for a hefty sum. He will not part with him cheaply for the Python is a man who drinks his own urine rather than water the soil with it. My friends, you need a break. Come and join me for a hot mug."

Over tea and the rough wheat balls of dough favored by mountain Tamangs, we told the old man, whose name was Hari Lama, about our elephant stable in Thakurdwara and our mission.

"Young Dilly and Nandu, I hope that you can purchase the Python's tusker for a fair price, if not perhaps steal it. I have never looked after an elephant, but I have raised many a yak and buffalo. If that tusker is not separated from its handlers, I fear it will die within weeks if not days."

"How much do you think he might want for it, *Shambo*?"

"The number is too big for me to know. But after he bought it, the villagers say he figured what it would cost him in upkeep, both for the animal and in salaries for the staff. And so, his interest in the creature vanished. It was then that he replaced the old drivers with new handlers, two brothers from Farzipur. Since their arrival a few months ago, the elephant has lost a lot of weight and can barely lift a log."

I heard my father once say that if you wanted to nurse a sick elephant back to strength, hire a Tharu from Simchi to care for it. If you wanted to kill it, hire a handler from Farzipur.

"The villagers suspected the brothers of stealing the elephant's rice ration and selling it in the bazaar. I have no proof, but anyone can see he is not well-fed."

"How much do you think he will want, *Shambo*?"

"I heard he bought the tusker for ninety thousand rupees. I doubt that he would accept a penny less."

"That much for a half-starved elephant?" I said. The old Tamang looked at my face, then turned to stare into the fire. A Tamang never likes to talk about what is hopeless.

We started back on the trail, which led out from the village to a small river. There we saw the Python's tusker cooling off in the river, submerged up to his head. A bearded man splashed water over the elephant and quickly ordered it out of the water. The tusker ignored him. The driver began beating the tusker about the head with his long stick until blood ran from its scalp.

Before Dilly could stop me, I ran up to the driver and spoke to him in Urdu. "They say an elephant lives to almost seventy years if he is treated well. If you beat him like a dog and refuse to bathe him properly, he may never reach his prime."

The man sneered at me and took a step forward to get closer to my face. "Perhaps it is not the fate of all elephants to live a long life. *Perhaps* it is none of your business."

And with another whack to the elephant's skull, the driver forced the animal out of the river. The elephant carried a huge set of ivory tusks, but his bones stuck out over his shoulders, and the points of his spine were visible along his back. The tusker's flanks were covered with open sores from beatings with the flat blade of the *khukri* carried by all elephant drivers. Streams of mucus trailed from the elephant's eyes.

I had to look away. The sight of this elephant made my heart hurt.

Dilly and I walked in silence for a long time. When we were too tired to walk any farther, we stopped for the night, just outside the city of Nepalganj. Early the next morning, we crossed into India and boarded the bus to Sonepur.

We would be six hours on the bus. I kept one hand over where I had hidden the leather satchel under my shirt and the other on the hilt of my *khukri*. Now I carried a real blade, a gift from my father made by the local blacksmith. But our fellow passengers posed no threat. Most were poor villagers who dragged their goats and lambs onto the bus with them. The others were too busy tending to their crying children to notice Dilly and me staring out the window.

They say Bihar is the poorest of Indian states, and the flat dusty scenery, with one sad, mud-walled village after another, certainly made it seem true. Clusters of houses were separated by barren fields of wheat stubble and dry pastures, with a sprinkle of skinny goats. A few acacias were scattered about, and the goats even nibbled on their thorny branches.

"What a strange place to hold an elephant fair. There is no decent patch of jungle for miles," I said to Dilly.

The bus bumped across the bridge that spans where the Ganges and the Gandaki River meet, and I thought of the Great Sand Bar River at home. Though it was so far away, some of its water would surely mingle with the Holy Ganges that flowed beneath us.

At last we reached the city. We dropped our tired legs down the stairs of the bus and set out to find the Sonepur bazaar.

TWENTY-FIVE

The trumpeting of the first-arriving elephants led us to the fairgrounds. We had arrived early, as my father had hoped, making it in time for the opening of the *Mela*.

It was like the Gularia bazaar only a hundred times bigger. The elephant arena was at the other end of the market, so we had to weave our way through row upon row of horses, donkeys, camels, and cattle, all for sale. It looked like a city of animals that far outnumbered the people. Hawkers had already set up their stalls on the edge of the viewing areas, selling food and drinks.

The sight of the first elephants made my heart race. There were dozens lined up in rows, with their handlers chatting away, touting the greatness of their animals to everyone, or to the air. With so many elephants already there, it was clear we were not early enough.

"Nandu, we are late," Dilly said, as if reading my mind. "We need a new plan. I think we should split up so we can get a look at all the elephants. We will meet in two hours to discuss the best ones."

"But *Subba-sahib* told us to stay together."

"We will be most of the time, Nandu. But first we need to see as many elephants as we can. If we stay together, one of the best ones might be sold before we even get a chance to see it. Let's meet up in two hours by the saddle makers' stalls."

Now on my own, one of the first buyers to catch my eye was an old man with a hunchback. He whispered to me, "You will be looking to purchase a great tusker."

I stared at his large grinning mouth with only three lower teeth left. "How do you know, Grandfather? Is it so obvious?"

"Since when does a handsome young man carrying a leather purse tucked under his arm come so far to buy chickens?" he cackled. "If you are looking for the best bargains, I can be of great assistance to you, for I once bought elephants for the Maharajah of Bihar."

"And why would you want to assist me?"

"A young man could be swindled of his money by those skilled in selling unhealthy elephants."

"But if you know so much about elephants, why are you skulking about instead of hawking your own elephants?"

The old man winced at my sharp language. "Hard times are upon us, my young friend, and the era of the great stables is passing. I must do what I can."

He paused. "Perhaps I can make you an offer. If I find you

an elephant for your price, you pay me five thousand rupees as a gift. If I fail, consider my labors to have been for free. This way you cannot lose. I know every seller at the fair and how far they will come down in bargaining."

I thought quickly about the hunchback's proposal. If he could guarantee me a fine tusker for sixty-five thousand or even seventy thousand rupees, I could find some way to pay an extra five thousand. My *khukri* was worth several thousand alone, and Dilly could sell his, too.

"I accept, Grandfather, but I warn you. I might look young, but I can smell a cheat as quickly as a bear smells his honey-comb."

Just then I saw Dilly approaching. He had returned in only fifteen minutes and looked upset.

"We do not have nearly enough rupees," he whispered.

I explained the old man's proposition. "We should do it, Dilly. He knows the fairground and the sellers."

Dilly shook his head but did not stop me from telling the old man more about our story. "I will tell you something else, Grandfather. We represent one of the finest stables in all of Nepal. We have come for a breeding tusker to service our females. But we have only sixty-five thousand and three hundred rupees to spend."

The old hunchback rolled his eyes and scuttled off.

"Wait!" I called. "What about our agreement?"

He walked back, so as not to shout.

"My young man, for that many rupees you can purchase only half a tusker. Which do you want to buy? The front end or the back end? Go back to your stable and fetch a stack of rupees. Then maybe I can help you."

"Please, Grandfather, it is all we have. We, too, have fallen on hard times." I quickly reeled off the story of the Thakurdwara stable's closing in only two months' time and our plan for a tusker.

"*Subba-sahib* has trained you well. If only he had stuffed your pockets with more money. Forget my commission, Nanda Singh, I will offer my services for free. Perhaps if you succeed with your breeding center, there will be a place for me."

"We will put in a good word with *Subba-sahib*," I said, glancing at Dilly, who still seemed unhappy with our new friend. "Lead us, Grandfather. May we ask your good name?"

"They call me Topsy. Now, lads, you must trust me and listen closely. With the sum that you carry, we have no chance of buying a tusker that has already reached the fairgrounds. They are priced far beyond your means. Our only hope is to approach elephant traders out along the Patna Road, before they have reached Sonepur, and try to strike a deal then and there. Perhaps a trader bringing many elephants would be happy to enter the bazaar with one sale under his belt. Let us not waste a moment, for the large caravans are near. Come, let us find you a great tusker that will bring glory to your stable, Nanda Singh."

"You may call me Nandu, Topsy, and we call Dil Bahadur, Dilly. Let's find our tusker."

We spotted the first approaching elephant caravan, followed by a cloud of dust. Dilly and I were forced to shorten our strides so that the old man could keep up with us. When we were close enough, Topsy immediately recognized the trader.

"The leader of this caravan is Moh-Mohat. He is one of the most famous elephant traders at Sonepur. They say that Moh-Mohat has bought and sold more than five hundred elephants in his time. He is an honest man, but shrewd. Few have ever bested him when it comes to dealing in elephant flesh."

"How did he earn the name Moh-Mohat, Topsy?" I asked.

"It is his way of speech. He stutters."

"*Salaam*, Moh-Mohat-*sahib*. Much elephant dung has dropped since we last met." Topsy bowed deeply to the elephant trader. The trader was riding a female whose head was painted in bright red and yellow.

"Gr-gr-greetings, you twisted old f-f-f-fart. Praise Allah that you are st-st-st-till alive, I see. What brings you out on the P-P-Patna Road? Why are you not at the *M-M-Mela*, p-p-peering into an elephant's anus?"

"The Great Trader still carries his humor like a camel carries its hump."

Moh-Mohat seemed unsure of what Topsy meant, but he laughed anyway.

"The truth is, my friends and I are interested in looking at tuskers. Might you have any in your caravan?" Topsy asked.

Jumma, Moh-Mohat's brother stepped forward. "If we

did, would my elder brother and I be riding these females into Sonepur? We, also, Topsy-*sahib* are looking to purchase a big male or two. They are getting harder to come by in Assam. I hear that Moti Lal and Jalaji will be bringing up some tuskers from the south. If this is true, you should meet them shortly."

"I hope that you carry a f-f-fat purse, my young fr-fr-friend," said Moh-Mohat, addressing me directly. "You will need it."

We kept walking. By late afternoon a second caravan appeared on the horizon. Topsy warned us, "Moti Lal, the leader of the caravan up ahead, is a fat thief and a vulgar excuse for a human being. A lot of wind comes out of both ends of this gasbag. I see little hope in dealing with him."

"Let us try, Topsy," I said, and I encouraged the old man to pick up our pace to meet the next trader. My stomach churned with nerves. I had no idea which scared me more, being robbed or not finding a tusker we could afford.

"Greetings, Moti Lal. You grow wider in girth with each *Mela*. Clearly wealth and rich buffalo milk over your rice agree with you."

"Praise Shiva. The Lord preserves the deformed and wicked as well as the righteous. What brings you out on the Patna Road, Topsy?"

"I will not delay the long journey of so famous a trader, Moti Lal. We seek a tusker. Rumor has it that you are bringing several to market. Can we see them before you show them off at the *Mela*?"

"You may inspect them, but I doubt you will be able to afford one. Maybe I could sell you some of their toenail shavings. I think those might be in your price range," guffawed the old man.

I felt my anger rise. But my anger was soon replaced by wonder when the *mahouts* drove the two huge males forward. I had never seen such powerful-looking elephants.

I could not stop my mouth from blurting out, "Moti Lal, we will give you sixty-five thousand and three hundred rupees right now for the smaller of the two tuskers or seventy thousand for the larger one."

Topsy again rolled his eyes at me. The fat trader let his jaw drop in mock horror. "You must teach your young friend how to bargain properly, Topsy-*sahib*."

Moti Lal turned to me, his jowels quivering. "Do not waste my time, young man, with an offer that is nothing more than a cumin seed in the mouth of an elephant."

After walking on in silence, Topsy finally spoke. "Nandu, I offer my services for free. Do not intercede unless I tell you to do so. Otherwise, you must continue without me."

"Forgive me, Topsy-*sahib*. It will not happen again. I am so desperate."

"Nothing comes of desperation, Nandu, except more misery. Keep a clear mind."

By now, the sinking sun had begun to show golden through the cloud of dust stirred up by yet another caravan. The shuffling elephants were strung out over several hundred yards on the Patna Road.

"Nandu and Dilly, this caravan is led by Jalaji and his brothers. Jalaji is mostly known as a trader in horses and camels, but now he is also bringing elephants to market for the second time in three years."

We counted twenty-two elephants in the caravan. "Topsy, there are enough elephants here to fill an entire stable," Dilly said.

"I think we have met our dealer. Now leave this to me," Topsy said. And Dilly gave me a look that said I had better be silent.

"Good evening, Jalaji. Word has traveled far ahead of you about the army of elephants you bring to Sonepur. Such a large caravan must have caused you much delay, for I know that all of the other traders have arrived, and half of their elephants have already been sold."

"If they have been sold once, then they may be sold again. When the merchants see the quality of my elephants, they will spark a bidding war, I promise you that. There is never an over-supply of good tuskers at the *Mela*."

"May we have a quick look at your animals, Jalaji? It will not take us long to see if your caravan has something to offer us."

"As you wish, but do not make me wait long. I have many elephants to sell, and I must return from Sonepur having sold every one."

"I understand your anxiety, Jalaji, and we will be quick. But if I may offer the advice of one who has traded at Sonepur for more than thirty years, I urge you to forget about selling all of your elephants at the *Mela*. If that was your plan, I would have brought no more than fourteen elephants rather than twenty-two."

Jalaji furrowed his brow and seemed nervous. Topsy had his attention. "What are you and your sons looking for, Topsy?"

"We are interested in a tusker."

"Go to the rear of the caravan. I keep them away from the females. There you will find three brave bulls."

Topsy ambled to the rear of the train of elephants, and Dilly and I followed him. He immediately began sizing up the three tuskers.

"Nandu and Dilly, the oldest male is a fine specimen but far beyond our price range. The second oldest is not bad looking, but his legs are too long and I am concerned by the odd shape of his spine. He is a sure bet for saddle sores. The smallest one is young, but he looks like he will become a fine tusker. We must pretend our real interest is in the oldest male, then we switch to the middle one, before we finally settle on the youngest. It may be our only hope."

"But the youngest is a teenager. It will be years before he can breed a female," Dilly said.

"It is the youngest bull, or nothing. It may still be nothing we can afford."

"So be it, Topsy-*sahib*," Dilly said.

I felt as disappointed as Dilly. We might not have years to wait to start our breeding center.

"Jalaji, you bring a tusker and two yearlings to market. Let us talk about your bull," started Topsy.

"Yes, old man, I bring three excellent bulls to market. Which one interests you?"

"Perhaps my eyes, which have examined thousands of elephants over the years, have finally begun to fail me. All I see is one mature tusker and two animals with tusks no longer than a man's thumb."

"How much are you willing to offer for the oldest male? You are trying my patience."

"If he was in his prime, I would offer a small fortune. But he is not a young animal and his toenails are ingrown and he does not walk straight. I can only offer you seventy thousand rupees."

"Do not insult me, Topsy. Perhaps we can discuss one of the other two elephants before us."

"Hardly worth discussing. The middle one has legs as tall as a *sal* tree and an odd disposition. It looks like he was poorly treated as a calf. I doubt he knows half the commands most elephants understand at his age. I would not raise my offer of seventy thousand rupees one penny for that lurching giraffe."

"Spare your compliments, old man, for I would not part with him for less than eighty thousand. If you have no interest in the young tusker, I must march on, for it will be well after dark by the time I reach Sonepur."

"You are a long way from Sonepur just as this young bull, a child among elephants, is far from becoming a breeding tusker. We will have to wait many years to decide what kind of elephant he will be, a real gamble indeed. I see bad bloodlines in the shape of his forehead and his eyes are too cloudy for my liking. One does not feel comfortable for a tusker to sport such a thick short trunk. He looks more like a buffalo with a feed bag attached to his head."

"Spare me, Topsy, for I have traveled far today and am quite weary. But I am not against the idea of selling an animal before I reach Sonepur. You are a lucky man. I will sell him to you for only seventy thousand rupees. Take it or leave it."

"For seventy thousand rupees, I could buy four camels that would do more work than this woeful insult to all that is grand in elephants. Sixty thousand is my only offer, and I cringe at even suggesting it."

"Go with God, old man. Go with God in search of camel dung, for that is all your meager offer will buy you."

"I am an old man and a fool, Jalaji. Yes, Topsy is a fool. Now, I will offer you sixty-five thousand rupees. It is a scandalous price for a tusker that would run at the sight of a dead chicken. It is my last quote, I cannot spare another penny, nor stare at him for too long."

"Consider it a deal. You can take charge of your tusker

tomorrow at the trader's stalls." Jalaji signaled for his younger brother to come forward with some papers. "Here is a temporary bill of sale." He took a seal from inside his jacket pocket and pressed it in wax his brother had ready and then stamped the paper. The young tusker was ours!

"You can trust that your money is as safe with me as with the Bank of Bombay," said Jalaji.

I spoke for the first time. "Here is a purse with your sum. We will see you tomorrow at the *Mela*."

After Jalaji had moved on, Topsy let out a cackle before putting his hand over his mouth.

"Someday, Dilly and Nandu, Jalaji will learn the true value of a tusker, but let us pray that day will come next year. Your new elephant would have brought at least eighty-five thousand at the *Mela*."

"Topsy, you must be tired from the walk. My back is strong and my legs are still fresh. Let me carry you back to Sonepur," I said.

"Many thanks, Nandu, but I will rest here tonight. Look, there is an old friend, Prem Lal, bringing his elephants to market. I will stay behind and talk with him. You go on to Sonepur. I will meet you early in the morning at Jalaji's stall."

"As you wish, Topsy, we'll take leave of you now. Thank you for all of your help."

Topsy bowed and offered his half grin. As we turned toward Sonepur, we heard him say, "Greetings, Prem Lal, my friend.

Your nose grows longer each time we meet. Can it be that your mother was half-elephant?"

I was smiling again, but not just because Topsy's way of speaking made me laugh. I thought of how happy my father would be when we led the new tusker into camp. His blessings had worked. At last, my fate was changing.

TWENTY-SIX

An elephant stable is a noisy place, but an elephant fairground is ten times as loud. As we approached the *Mela*, we heard hundreds of elephants roar, moan, trumpet, snort, and fart. It was like entering another world.

"Nandu, do you remember what Ramji says, 'How lucky elephants are. They are the only creatures allowed to fart in front of the king without going to jail for it'?" We both laughed and then headed outside the fairgrounds, where it was quieter, to spread out our bedrolls for the night.

Crowing roosters woke Dilly and me. We got up and walked through the bazaar looking for tea and biscuits. "I had a strong dream last night," I said. "We had found our elephant and were on our way back home to Thakurdwara. But instead of walking, our tusker flew through the air and landed in front of *Subba-sahib*'s bungalow."

"That is good luck," Dilly said, handing rupees to the seller in the tea stall.

213

"Only one problem," I said. "The tusker was not the young male we purchased last night."

"It was just a dream. Not all the details matter. Now let's drink our tea quickly. We are to meet Jalaji at his stall."

But our seller was gone. He had left before dawn, after hearing news that one of his camel caravans had been held up by bandits along the border.

"Here is something for you," said Dep, Jalaji's brother. He reached into his robe and pulled out our satchel of money. "I believe you will find your rupees intact. Count it if you like."

"I do not understand. We purchased his youngest tusker. I have the papers. Where is our elephant?" I cried.

Dep continued. "I am afraid that my brother sold it last night to a trader from Gujarat for ninety thousand rupees. When we arrived at Sonepur and realized how much tuskers were going for, my brother became angry. He said that Topsy had pulled a fast one on him."

"But we made a deal. You cannot break your word!"

"It is not my word, young fellow. I am sorry for you, but I am unable to influence the mind of my eldest brother. But to show you that he meant well, Jalaji added five thousand rupees to your sixty-five thousand. Consider it one night's interest. Now you have more to spend than when you started out. Good day, sirs, and good luck."

Dilly and I walked away. There was nothing to be done. Even Dilly could find no words to make the situation brighter. We were returning five thousand rupees richer but having failed in our quest.

"It was clearly not our fate to buy this elephant. I saw it in my dream," I said. On the way out of the bazaar, we passed a row of astrologers, palm readers, and men hawking exotic live animals and folk medicines. A merchant with dark, wrinkled skin and a mustache like a scorpion's tail caught my eye.

"You are interested in some barking deer antler, my friend?" he asked. "Grind up the antler, put it in your wife's rice, and she will bear you many sons. It is written in the Vedas."

"No thank you, I have no desire to buy your antlers or your birds, except possibly to free them."

"Perhaps this other creature will interest you." The merchant reached into a wicker basket and hauled out a huge python. "He will keep the rats out of your granary."

"I already know about one python worse than this one. I will deal with him first." The cold yellow eyes of the snake peered at me, and I returned the serpent's stare.

We would bring an elephant home. I had seen it in my dream. And there was only one elephant I knew of between Sonepur and Thakurdwara.

———

Gobrechar emerged up ahead through the morning mist. During our long trip, Dilly and I discussed the landlord's tusker. We had nothing to lose and decided that we should approach the Python with an offer.

"I watched Topsy persuade Jalaji that his most prized elephants were of less value. I know I can do it," I told Dilly.

"So you think you can outwit the Python?"

"Yes, I will tell him that his tusker has the black tongue and that only a healer like *Subba-sahib* would have a chance at curing him. And even that is far from certain. I will offer to take the dying tusker off his hands for sixty thousand rupees."

"Okay, Topsy Singh," Dilly said, laughing. "Let's do it."

Dilly and I scaled a mango tree. It overlooked the Python's orchard and courtyard. Together, they were the size of our entire elephant stable. The Python was indeed a very rich man. We waited until it was dark. The Python would be well-fed after dinner and in what I hoped would be a good mood.

The moon was coming up. The two bearded handlers entered the far corner of the courtyard and threw the tusker a handful of chopped banana stems and a few *kuchis* wrapped in banana leaves.

"That is not enough food for an elephant calf, Nandu," Dilly whispered.

We waited. It seemed the Python only sat for his dinner at around ten o'clock like a lot of wealthy people. My legs ached from crouching, but we kept our eyes on the elephant, who was chained by his front legs to a post in the ground.

I rehearsed my speech once more, softly under my breath,

then we began to climb down. "Wait," Dilly whispered. "Someone is coming."

Below us, a figure slipped out of the shadows and eased over the wall into the courtyard.

"Nandu, did you see that man? He was wearing a bandana. Maybe he is going to rob the Python. Forget bargaining. We should steal off with the tusker while we have the chance," Dilly whispered.

We held off and waited, but the man did nothing. Finally, he slipped through the back gate of the courtyard. The elephant let out a deep rumble. "That is the sound of a starving elephant," I whispered to Dilly.

The tusker rattled his chains, but his handlers did not come.

"Nandu, did you see that?" Dilly asked.

"See what, Dilly?" I had shifted my eyes to a figure moving inside the house. The Python's shadow slithered across the window panes.

"Look at the elephant!" Dilly said. "I swear I saw the *muti* in his forehead."

I looked back to see the tusker bobbing its head as elephants do when they beg for food from their handlers. When he swung his head again toward us and into the moonlight, a spot glowed in his forehead like a diamond.

"I see it, Dilly! It is a sign!" We shinnied down the tree and were over the wall in seconds.

While Dilly found a hiding place in one of the remaining

shadows in the courtyard, I walked up to the house and knocked loudly on the door.

The Python looked at me with surprise when he opened it. "Who dares to knock at this hour?"

"Your Grace, it is late, but I only disturb you in a matter of urgency. I am from the Thakurdwara elephant stable. I am Nanda Singh, *mahout*."

"And what does a *mahout* want with me so late?"

"To speak with you for just a few minutes of your valuable time."

The Python stepped back and allowed me to enter into the large entry room of his house. The door closed heavily behind me. Inside, the air was cool, the ceilings high, like a palace.

"Your Grace, I swear to you that your elephant will not live two more months. He will die here in your courtyard without treatment. If you allow it, I will make you a fair offer and take him to a healer."

"What you tell me is most disturbing. As you can see, I am not a *Subba-sahib*, I am a landowner who knows little about elephants. Yet, my friend who gave me this creature as a gift, he paid a small fortune for him, I am told, and thus, I am loathe to part with him."

I knew the Python was lying. The old village Tamang had told us that the landowner had purchased the tusker for himself.

I played my second card. "Your Grace, you remember the old saying, 'If you have an enemy, give him the gift of an elephant.

At first he will be most appreciative of the grand gesture. A year later, he will rue the day he accepted it as the elephant eats him out of house and home.' "

"They do indeed eat a lot and require good care. I have two *mahouts* I brought all the way from Farzipur to look after him."

"Your Grace, I must be honest, we have passed by this way twice in the past month and noticed the poor health of your tusker. Why does he bob his head and cry out so?"

The Python shook his own large head. "I do not know. Is that not natural for an elephant?"

"If I may say, your *mahouts* do their job poorly. They appear to be starving him to death."

The landlord did not react.

"Your Grace, if I may inquire, what is his daily rice ration? How much grass is he fed?"

The Python said nothing. Our conversation had taken a turn for the worse.

"Your Grace, we are not wealthy, but we offer you fifty thousand rupees for your elephant. That is all we have." It amazed me how easily the lie slipped off my tongue.

"I will need some time to consider your offer. Let me think it over for a day or so, and I will send word of my decision."

By that time, I thought, these Farzipur butchers might starve the elephant to death. Before I could think of a reply, we heard blood-curdling shrieks coming from the courtyard.

TWENTY-SEVEN

The powerful scent of night-flowering jasmine and gardenias filled the courtyard. The two great vessels holding the flowers had been knocked over in the corner where the elephant was tethered. I crept behind the water fountain to get a better look, with the Python following close on my heels. In the moonlight, we could see a body, motionless, lying against the tree.

The starving elephant had attacked one of the handlers. In front of us, the elephant began to roar.

Dilly yelled for me to take cover.

Suddenly, the elephant lunged toward us, yanking his tethering post in one pull from the ground. I could not think, I did not think, I just held out my wrist with the amulet made from Devi Kali's hair, and shouted, *"Raa!"*

The elephant stopped in its tracks, but he was still rumbling in anger. The second handler sat hunched in a ball, panicking. The elephant turned away from me and swung his trunk, knocking the other handler through the air. He landed with a thud.

"*Chii!*" I shouted, and the elephant stopped and left the body where it was. My arm was still raised, frozen in the air. The elephant took in a deep breath and grew quieter, rumbling a little, his dark gray skin twitching. He moved toward me again and lifted his trunk.

"He will kill you, too," the Python whispered. "He will kill us all." The Python crouched in what seemed like prayer.

But I could sense that the elephant was not attacking. He lifted his trunk, and I could hear the air moving in and out of it. The tusker stepped closer and closer toward my wrist until the tip of his trunk was touching and smelling the bracelet. I felt his breath against my skin. Then he curled the tip of his trunk into his mouth, as if there were something in it, something good to eat, and let out a soft rumble.

I dropped my hand. Dilly threw me a banana stem he had picked up in the courtyard, and I walked toward the enormous elephant, all the while talking softly and offering him food. He was starving and took it. I inched closer and closer, whispering kind words, but then the elephant swung his head toward the Python. I stepped out of the way. The tusker spread his ears, ready to charge.

He took two steps forward, still dragging the tethering post behind him.

"Stop him, Nanda Singh," the Python screamed. "Stop him!"

I hesitated only a second then yelled, *"Raa!"*

The elephant stopped, but, with his ears wide, almost like wings, he remained ready to attack. I stepped between the elephant and the Python. I do not know what made me so bold, but I turned to look the Python straight in the eye and said, "We will take this tusker at a price of fifty thousand rupees. Not one penny more."

"Yes, yes, just take him away. Now!" he pleaded.

"We will need an official bill of sale. Without one, someone can say that this elephant was stolen."

"Yes, yes, I will have it all prepared by morning. Send your *Subba-sahib* tomorrow, and it will be made legal."

One handler let out a moan. The other, under the tree, still had not moved. We cut some stems of banana from the orchard to feed to our brave tusker and led him out of the courtyard.

In the dark night, we turned onto the Gularia Road. We were on our way home. Our new tusker walked slowly beside us. He was weak and had to stop nearly every half mile to rest.

"Hold on, my friend, for soon you will be home, and *Subba-sahib* will make you strong again," I said to him.

"I hope it is even possible for the *Subba-sahib* to make him well," Dilly said. "Nandu, you must never tell anyone, but I made the tusker charge. Those handlers were not just starving the elephant. I think they were going to poison him to death and make off with the tusks."

I reached out my hand and held it against the elephant's belly as he walked beside me. "How do you know?" I asked. My voice came out as a whisper.

"I watched them mix a powder in with the rice for the *kuchis* from a packet. And then they used a dropper to add some liquid. I had never seen *Subba-sahib* treat any of our elephants like that. It had to be poison, not medicine, I thought.

"I had to act fast. If that elephant stayed one more night, he would be dead by tomorrow. I had no knowledge if the tusker understood any commands, but I shouted as loud as I could, *'Hikh! Hikh!'* hoping he would attack."

"He did," I said, still holding my hand against the tusker's side.

"I found *this* while you were talking to the Python just before we left."

"What is it, Dilly?"

"Rat poison," he said, holding up an empty packet. "One of the Farzipurs dropped it."

"Do you think the Python knew?"

"I think so, yes. Maybe they were planning to double-cross him, once the elephant was dead, and make off with the tusks."

We walked for some time in silence. A breeze streamed gently into our faces, which seemed just cool enough to keep us awake. I could barely wait to help mend the tusker. He looked so awful now, but I knew with our care he would become an elephant as strong and brave and noble as Devi Kali.

"Do you think that everyone will see the value in our tusker? I do not want the other drivers to judge him harshly now, because he looks so beaten down."

"Do not worry, *Subba-sahib* can look deep inside. He will know that this is a brave animal. We will tell him the story. We have seen his courage and his ability to follow commands—he has been well-trained—and that was when he was nearly out of his mind with hunger and pain."

Dilly knew his elephants, and I was relieved that he sensed the same qualities that I did.

"Nandu, what will you name him?" Dilly asked, trying to speak of happier things.

"I will call him Hira Prashad, because we saw his *muti*, shining like a diamond in the moonlight."

"Yes," Dilly said, resting his hand on my shoulder. "I will never forget it."

We three walked on linked together, hand to elephant, hand to shoulder.

Hira Prashad's fate was now one with mine.

We were almost home. When we rounded the last bend near Thakurdwara, the sun peeked out from the edge of the forest. I could make out my father's bungalow, then the gazebo and the other stable buildings.

"Hira Prashad, just ahead is the stable," I said to my new friend. "You will be most welcome. *Subba-sahib* and I will treat your gashes, and you will grow strong again. I will cut you branches from the tastiest figs. You will eat like a king of the jungle—which you are."

Hira Prashad could barely move another step. "Come, Hira Prashad, just a little farther, and there will be fresh grass for your breakfast. Then you can sleep all day."

From far off I could see my father slowly making his way toward us on the road, leaning on a walking stick. He could not wait, even with his gout. Behind him, at the entrance to the stable, the drivers gathered at the gate. Even from far away in the early morning light, they could see it was a male, so large and white were his tusks.

The sun had begun to slant its rays through the trees, when my father reached us. Before he could say anything, I began quickly to tell the whole story.

"Nandu, slow down! Your tongue flaps faster than a sunbird's wings." My father circled around the elephant without saying anything. At last he stopped, leaned on his cane, and looked face-to-face with the tusker.

"Hmmm, I see the fresh wounds on his scalp and head. This must have been the work of some cruel handlers." I felt my heart sink.

He paused and started humming.

"But I also see a great tusker before me. Nandu, you and Dilly have done very well. When I look deep inside him, I see courage in his heart. I see intelligence and loyalty in his eyes. To find such a splendid animal, we could not have hoped for more."

I looked at Dilly and he winked back at me. We were both too tired to speak.

"He is indeed a proud tusker, but he has not been treated like one. Come, Hira Prashad, I will fix you up. By tomorrow, my salves will stop the oozing from your eyes. In two weeks, my poultices will heal your wounds. In three months, you will be breeding our females."

By this time, all the other drivers had joined us. One by one, they came up, bowed to us, then saluted our new tusker.

"Welcome home, Nandu and Dilly. Bless you, Hira Prashad," said Phirta.

"All hail Nandu and Dilly! All hail Hira Prashad!" shouted Joker.

"For fifty thousand rupees, *Subba-sahib*, to purchase such a promising tusker, the *mahouts* deserve a toast," said Sukh, who had hardly spoken ten words to me in months.

As much as I craved my father's approval, the words of praise from the old drivers—Phirta, Joker, Sukh, and Ramji—made me glow with pride. I had to choke back my tears not to embarrass myself in front of my father. The same head drivers who had shunned me ever since I had thrown my hand ax at the tigress and defied the king, the ones who blamed me for our great misfortune, now welcomed me back. At last, I felt I had redeemed myself in their eyes. I was one of them again, or perhaps one of them for the first time.

"Tonight we must celebrate. The Conservator-*sahib* will listen to us now," said *Subba-sahib*.

Hira Prashad began to rumble. Maybe it was his intense hunger speaking, but I am quite sure it was more likely happiness at finding his home.

PART V
THE DHOLE MAKE A DISCOVERY

TWENTY-EIGHT

Waving the bill of sale over his head, *Subba-sahib* called the drivers together.

"Hira Prashad is ours," he announced. I felt the chills run down my spine again, just like when Dilly and I led the tusker into our stable.

"There is another letter you need to hear, drivers," said *Subba-sahib*, "the letter I just dictated to Nandu. Read it out loud, *mahout*."

"To the conservator of forests, the Borderlands," I began. "Please note that we have found a strong tusker to start our breeding center. He will produce many fine elephants in the future. We ask that you consider our proposal to remain in Thakurdwara to take on this new role. Please share this with the Palace Wildlife Committee. Humbly, Kumar Lotan, *Subba-sahib*, Officer-in-Charge, Thakurdwara."

"Now we have a real tusker. The conservator-*sahib* has to give us a second chance," said Ramji.

Just in case Watermelon Belly was still not on our side, my father told me that he would send another copy of the letter and proposal to his friend at the palace.

But I did not dwell long on the fate of my father's letters. I had the job of caring for Hira Prashad, who was still too weak to carry his own fodder. Dilly and I made two trips a day on Man Kali to cut fig branches and *baruwa* grass for him. I built a small lean-to near his tethering post, where I could watch him all night if I wanted to.

I was not his only caretaker. My father tended to Hira Prashad like the royal elephant he was. He applied poultices to draw the infection out of his many wounds. I helped him change the bandages four times a day. After just two weeks in our care, my father was pleased with our tusker's progress.

"It is a miracle this elephant did not die, Nandu," he said to me, as I stood by with long torn strips of clean cloth hung along my outstretched arm. I watched them flutter and dance in the breeze.

"Fortunately," he continued, "we have plenty of food for him. An extra dose of crude sugar and salt in his *kuchis* will help, too."

Help what? I wondered. My father had seen something else, too, when he looked straight into Hira Prashad's eyes, but he was not telling me.

I also wanted Hira Prashad to put on weight. Each night

I asked for extra rice from Tulsi, who would joke with me, "Nandu, you eat for two men now. Your trip to India must have doubled your hunger."

I would nod and smile. The truth was I would divide my rice, leave a handful for myself, then stuff the rest into an extra *kuchi* for Hira Prashad.

"His ribs are already less visible," I said to my father, brushing my hand along the side of his belly.

"Indeed. I am no longer worried about his recovery. He has a strong frame and will be a magnificent tusker in six months' time."

Hira Prashad's strength grew. He devoured his *kuchis*, then swung his trunk in giant circles, telling me he was ready for more. We tethered him to the same post where Devi Kali stood. This time, when the full moon shone bright on the stable, the spot was no longer empty. I felt Devi Kali watching over him. How she would have welcomed Hira Prashad to the stable, after all that we had been through to bring him here.

When the rhino calves were asleep, Rita sometimes came to the lean-to to sit with me. Hira Prashad lay on his side and let out a deep sigh. He still slept more than the other elephants. I wished his *muti* would flash once more in the moonlight, so that Rita could see it, too.

"You have done a great thing, Nandu," she said. "You and Dilly brought home a beautiful tusker."

"I think he will be the finest in the Borderlands," I said. "I hope our plan works."

Rita smiled at me. I had never noticed before how pretty she looked, especially in the moonlight.

"If *Subba-sahib* would let me, I know I could drive Man Kali, too, like Dilly. I wish I could be a boy just so I could drive an elephant. I know they would respond to me," she said. "But at least Father Autry treats me the same as a boy. I have been practicing my English with him. He says I am supremely talented."

She said the words "supremely talented" in English, perfectly imitating Father Autry.

"Rita, you are very talented, especially with wild animals. The rhinos are like puppies around you. When the elephant calves are born here, you will be the one to look after them, not me or Dilly. There will be no role more important in the stable."

Her dark eyes flashed at me.

Hira Prashad let out another sigh in his sleep.

"Do you think he knows that you and Dilly saved his life?" Rita asked.

"*Subba-sahib* says that what elephants know is greater than we can imagine. I think Hira Prashad smelled danger, but he was too weak to escape on his own."

His great tusks glowed under the light of the full moon.

"Do you think he is dreaming?"

"Yes," I said. "Look how his skin quivers. Maybe he is dreaming about his herd in a field of lemongrass, under a gentle rain."

Hira Prashad snorted softly.

I looked at Rita. She had started to breathe like Hira Prashad, exhaling loudly followed by a long slow inhale. I started to do the same. Rita looked at me and there we sat, breathing in and out with our elephant, while the rest of the stable slept.

TWENTY-NINE

"Dilly, I wish old Topsy could see our tusker now!"

"Nanda Singh, I will give you seventy thousand rupees for this half-hippopotamus, not a penny more," Dilly said, mimicking our friend from Sonepur. Even just riding Hira Prashad, we could feel the tusker's growing strength. He was packing on so much muscle, you could hardly tell that he had been starved for so long.

Both *Subba-sahib* and I were admiring him near the open-air part of the stable. The other drivers were out grazing the elephants or taking the day off like Dilly. We had brought Hira Prashad in to measure him for a new saddle. On the wall hung Devi Kali's old one as a memorial. No elephant would ever use it again.

Hira Prashad walked up to her saddle and began rubbing his trunk over it.

"*Chhi*," I told him, ordering him to leave it alone, lest it fall off its hook. For the first time ever, Hira Prashad ignored me and kept rubbing his trunk over and over and snorting softly. *"Chhi!"* I commanded again. *"Subba-sahib*, he is not listening to me."

"He has good reason not to. Let him be. He is acquainted with the elephant that once wore this saddle."

"But how?"

"Nandu, come sit here and I will share with you a story. It is one you must never repeat to anyone, or it will mean the end of the stable for sure."

Somehow the words sounded so much like the Baba's request, when he told me his dark secret about his past. "I will tell no one, Father."

"Twenty-five years ago, ten years after I came to this stable, a wild bull elephant came through the Borderlands and impregnated two of our females when they were out grazing. Ramji saw it happen. One of the females was Devi Kali and the other was Laxmi Kali. Both sired calves, and Devi Kali gave us a healthy male."

"Yes, Father, I knew that she had given birth to a female calf. It is now at the Chitwan stable. But I did not know about the male."

"Nandu, the palace never paid much attention to us and in some years, we received almost no stipend at all. We had to scrape by and could barely afford the rice ration for the elephants. That year there was famine across much of the mountain villages, and our budget was taken away to help those who went hungry. I realized that our stable would go under if I did not do something drastic. So this, you must tell no one."

"I swear on Devi Kali's grave."

"I sold Devi Kali's male calf to a landowner in Kailali and Laxmi Kali's female calf to a landlord in Kanchanpur District. Only Ramji knows of this, and he would never say anything. If word got back to the palace that I had sold royal elephants, I would be dismissed immediately and even jailed."

I stared at the ashes in the fire. Now I knew the other reason why my father could never dismiss Ramji. He shared my father's secret.

"When I read the bill of sale for Hira Prashad, I noticed that the Python had purchased him from a landlowner in Kailali District. It was the same man that I had sold the male calf to twenty-five years ago. Nandu, I was almost certain that Devi Kali is Hira Prashad's mother, but now, seeing him rub his trunk against her saddle, and the way he responded to your bracelet from her tail hairs, I am sure."

THIRTY

A male spotted deer eyed a rival buck. They lifted their heads in display, then slammed into each other. The sound of clashing antlers echoed across the open meadow where I was grazing Hira Prashad. Dilly was with me on Man Kali.

"They will fight and spar until they settle who is the boss. Then the winner will drive the other males away from the females," Dilly said.

Our elephant stable was no different. Several older females vied to be matriarch after Devi Kali's passing. But the arrival of Hira Prashad changed life for them. The other elephants quickly gave way to him, and he became the undisputed king. Even the *phanits*, the old drivers, took notice. And though I was still a lowly *mahout*, I was the only one Hira Prashad would really allow to drive him.

Here was the problem. Ramji was no longer fit to drive an elephant, let alone a tusker. And my father could not promote me to be *phanit*, the head driver, at my age. No driver in the stable would respect that decision, but at the same time no one volunteered to drive Hira Prashad. Everyone except Dilly, my father, and me was afraid to ride him.

My father took me aside. "We must promote Sukh to *phanit*. And you must help him get used to the tusker."

The honor of being named head driver sat poorly with Sukh. His fear of Hira Prashad showed from the moment he climbed up the tusker's back. When elephants are unhappy with their driver, the most ornery ones will attempt to shake them—or anyone else riding—off the saddle. Several times, right in the stable, Hira Prashad tried to throw Sukh from his back, honking and roaring. The tusker only calmed down when I rushed over and stroked his trunk.

My father gave Sukh and me clear instructions about the danger of handling a tusker. "Once a male reaches fifteen, most healthy tuskers with females in their midst will enter *musth*. If our Hira Prashad shows signs of it, you must alert me at once. They are the most dangerous then to females and to their handlers."

I had seen our older male, Mahendra Gajh, in *musth*. He first began to leak fluid from his temples. Then he became pushy towards females and had to be separated. *Subba-sahib* had put a loud cowbell around his neck to warn anyone in his path of his approach.

I joined Sukh to take Hira Prashad to the jungle across the

Belgadi River. Sukh was driving but even with me also riding, the tusker started acting up again. Rather than calm him, Sukh whacked Hira Prashad hard several times with the flat end of his hand ax.

"Stop!" I screamed at him. "He will never listen to you that way."

"Get off my elephant and walk back home. I do not need you to tell me how to drive a tusker, you dung sweeper," Sukh said. "You are nothing but bad luck for the stable."

Sukh shoved me off the elephant and whacked Hira Prashad again. The elephant roared and began to run off. I did not walk back to the stable, but instead climbed a *kadam* tree in the middle of the meadow. "I will tell *Subba-sahib* what happened," I heard myself say out loud. I would not stand for anyone mistreating Hira Prashad. He had suffered enough for several lifetimes.

I watched as Hira Prashad slowed down and moved his trunk back and forth, like he was looking for something. Then I heard Sukh screaming and the next thing I knew an angry swarm of bees was attacking them. It looked like Hira Prashad had stepped on a bee's nest in the ground on purpose.

The swarm went after them, stinging them both over and over, until my tusker reached the Belgadi River and went underwater to escape the stings. Sukh was not so lucky. He was stung and stung, and by the time I got to him, his face was beet red and swollen like a melon. I pulled him over my shoulders to carry home. Fortunately, we met Phirta leading Prem Kali to the river. We turned her around, loaded Sukh on her back, and rushed him to camp.

"*Subba-sahib,*" I called. "You must come at once! Hira Prashad has thrown Sukh. They were attacked by bees."

Two of the drivers loaded Sukh into the oxcart to haul him to Thakurdwara, where there was a nurse. I hoped he would live. Some people die from bee stings in the Borderlands—especially when there are so many.

In minutes, five elephants had been saddled, with my father on Mel Kali in the lead. All of the elephants carried thick ropes in case we had to restrain Hira Prashad. "Come, *mahout*, we need you. Climb up here."

I shouted to Mel Kali, "*Khol beit!*" and she stepped forward and leaned her trailing legs back so I could shinny up to the saddle. Once I was seated, the elephant took off and headed down the trail to the Belgadi River.

"If Hira Prashad is full of stingers, he will be most irritated. We must approach carefully. Nandu, he could act the same as a wild elephant."

Under *Subba-sahib's* command, the five elephants spread out once they crossed the river.

Hira Prashad had left broken branches in his wake and had even knocked down a small tree, so it was easy to track him. We spotted him below a *dubdube* tree, on the ground, rubbing his back against the trunk to try and remove the stingers. When he heard the other elephants approach, Hira Prashad rumbled in anger.

"*Subba-sahib*, I will approach him alone. I think he trusts me."

"Nandu, he may trust no one after all that has happened. You must be extremely careful."

I dropped off the elephant while my father was still speaking. I had already devised a plan back at the stable, when I noticed something about Mel Kali. She, too, was ready to breed. So I approached her and said, "Excuse me, Mel Kali, for being so bold, but you must help me bring our tusker back." I took off the Devi Kali hair bracelet I always wore, and swiped it several times between the skin on her legs so that it would be filled with the scent of a female elephant.

I slowly approached the tusker and stopped a few feet in front of him. I could see the swollen lumps from the bee stings.

"Hira Prashad, it is me, Nandu. I am here to protect you, just as when I found you in the Python's courtyard. Come, here is a message from Mel Kali. Soon you will be ready to be with her."

I held up my wrist so the elephant could catch the aroma. Hira Prashad stopped rumbling and lifted his trunk. "Please, Hira Prashad, come back to our stable. Sukh is very sorry for what he did." And then I made a decision that was not mine to make, but I felt I had to say it, to get Hira Prashad back. "He will never drive you again. I am the only one who will do so from now on."

I was now only three feet from the tusker. I waited. Then

Hira Prashad lifted his trunk and touched the tip to the bracelet, put the tip in his mouth, and let out a gentle rumble.

I pulled out my *khukri*. Using the flat part of the metal blade, I gently pressed it against the elephant's skin around the stingers. The heat from the sting is conducted through the blade and released. I remembered how my father had soothed my own pain with his blade when I had been stung.

I moved the flat knife around Hira's body, finally climbing on to his back to reach the stingers on his forehead. It was working. The tusker let out a deep rumble of contentment. The five females now standing around him rumbled back. Using the tweezers we carry in our driver's satchel to remove thorns, I plucked out as many stingers as I could see. Hira Prashad had calmed to the point where he let me sit behind his neck and drive him.

Our tusker was ready to come home.

I followed behind the other elephants. When we were out of hearing range, I leaned down to Hira Prashad's ear and whispered, "Thank you, Hira Prashad, for your trust. Now, we must go back and save our stable."

———

I was still thinking about my tusker while I was standing on the veranda of Father Autry's bungalow, about to enter and resume my lessons. I pushed my anger at Sukh below the surface.

"Nandu, welcome, welcome. Do come in," said Father Autry.

I was greeted by the smile of my teacher and remembered what I wanted to say. "Father-*sahib*, I have some good news."

Father Autry's face brightened and his deep blue eyes began to sparkle.

"We have a paradise flycatcher's nest in the lemon tree at the stable. I have been guarding the nest from the mongoose who come to steal her eggs. We will have nestlings soon."

"That is wonderful to hear. I am sure the mother bird is grateful for your protection."

I told Father Autry the other news, too, about how Sukh had treated Hira Prashad so harshly.

"It is a wonder the tusker did not pull Sukh off and trample him," Father Autry said.

"I must tell you, Father, about my conversation with the *Subba-sahib*. I said that Sukh will never drive Hira Prashad again."

"That is very bold, Nandu," the Father said.

"Yes, Father-*sahib*, I know. I also said I will be his only driver."

"And what did the *Subba-sahib* say?"

"He put his hand on my shoulder and said, 'Come my young *phanit*, I need a *raksi*.' "

THIRTY-ONE

The chill of late November sent the birds south to the Malabar coast of India and our elephant drivers closer to the campfire's edge. I went to deliver firewood to the Baba so he could stay warm. When Hira Prashad and I approached, the Baba walked toward us waving happily. I commanded the tusker to sit down next to the woodpile. The Baba and I watched as the elephant's thick back legs bent and folded under him, his body descending like a giant tent to cover them. Then I unloaded the split pieces of *sal* wood stacked on the saddle.

While my elephant was still relaxed on the ground, the Baba put his hand on the tusker's trunk and gave it a loving pat. The elephant replied with a short, soft snuffle and stood up.

"Baba, he dislikes most people coming too close, but not you. I can tell. He feels deep affection for you." The Baba bowed to Hira Prashad.

The Baba whispered, "You have brought enough firewood

for one hundred *sadhus*. I am most grateful. Come into my hut for tea." I had grown used to the Baba's soft voice, which he continued to use less and less. He seemed to always try to find another way to communicate; usually it was just a look in his eyes that was sometimes followed by a little jump of his eyebrows. For being as old as he was, his eyes were clear, and I could feel that they took in more than other men's did.

While the Baba tended his pot, Hira Prashad stood alone at the forest edge and rubbed his backside against the bark of a nearby tree, which made the upper branches shudder and shake. Large flakes peeled off as he scratched. Then he picked up a stick with his trunk and rubbed the point of it against the inside of his front leg.

"Your tusker is a very proud elephant. I am sure he will be the breeder *Subba-sahib* was hoping to find. And he makes you very happy, I see."

"Baba, in the jungle, I cannot believe his strength and intelligence. We are already very close, but I care for him differently from the way I felt about Devi Kali. Completely different. It is hard to describe."

"Words are not needed, Nandu. I read the Sanskrit texts all day long. But listening to the birds singing and the animals calling brings me greater calm than reciting verses."

I could tell the Baba had not spoken this much in quite some time. His voice was getting softer and softer.

"My dear friend, there is something I must say now that is hard to say."

"Please tell me, Baba. I will keep your secret."

"This is no secret. But this is the last time we will speak."

"What do you mean, Baba?" I sputtered. "Are you ill?"

"No, I am fine, my friend. You know that I speak very seldom. It is my way of showing God that I have so much to learn about compassion and awareness, and, if I am talking all the time, I cannot hear what is important. But now I have decided to give my tongue entirely to Lord Krishna. I no longer need to speak in this world."

The Baba saw the look of hurt on my face. "But do not worry, my fondness for you will always be visible, my friend, even if you do not hear the words." And with that, the Baba stood and hugged me. We walked in silence to the clearing where Hira Prashad was waiting patiently, and the Baba watched as I climbed onto my saddle. He waved to us, then turned away and walked into his temple, into his life of silence.

I went through Thakurdwara on the way home. I needed time to ponder the Baba's vow and how it made me feel—which was a mixture of sadness and wonder. At the edge of the village, the children gathered when they saw us coming. They loved to watch the giant tusker, even though they were too scared to get close.

Hira Prashad stepped gallantly along the road, kicking up small puffs of dust. I noticed a boy standing there who looked to be Dilly's age, eighteen or so. He did not flinch when we came inches away from where he stood. Even more surprising was that

Hira Prashad stayed completely calm, even swinging his trunk into the air to take in his scent.

"*Raa,*" I commanded Hira Prashad, and he stopped directly next to the boy, still searching the air with the end of his trunk, as if gathering more samples that might reveal something more about this calm Tharu standing in the grass.

"*Ram, Ram,*" I greeted him in the Tharu dialect.

"*Ram, Ram.* I have been watching you on your magnificent tusker for a week now. You seem young to handle such a powerful elephant."

"Yes, I am only a *pachuwa*, but as *Subba-sahib* says, 'a proud tusker chooses his driver, not the other way round.'"

"I believe it," he said.

Then to my surprise he stepped closer and laid his hand on the side of Hira Prashad's belly. It seemed foolish to take such a risk, but Hira Prashad did nothing. In fact, he dropped his trunk and began searching the side of the road for grass. I had never seen him so calm with a stranger.

"What is your name?" I asked.

"Indra. I am the cousin of Hala Ram, visiting from Gobrela. Do you think it would be possible for me to ride with you a while? Back to the stable? I have always dreamed of being an elephant driver. Literally. I have dreamed it."

Indra had never been on an elephant, but Hira Prashad took to him right away. As we rode down the Gularia Road, there was no change in the elephant's mood. He was as peaceful as if I were the only one driving him. And I thought to myself, It appears that Hira Prashad has chosen his own *mahout*, as well.

We rode straight into the stable grounds. The drivers were sitting around having their afternoon tea and stopped to stare at the young man who had joined me atop Hira Prashad. My father stepped out from his office near the canteen and looked up at us. He seemed pleased, though he did not smile.

I commanded Hira Prashad to lower himself so Indra and I could dismount. Then Dilly came to lead the elephant out to the edge of the forest, where he would feed him some fig branches and extra *kuchis*.

"You must introduce me to your friend," said my father.

"*Subba-sahib*, this is Indra, cousin of Hala Ram. He is most keen to work with elephants, and as you see, Hira Prashad likes him already."

"Indeed."

"Yes, sir," said Indra. "It is true that I wish more than anything to work in the stable. I know I must start as a stable hand, and I am ready and willing."

"Come back tomorrow morning, and I will let you know of my decision," my father said.

"Thank you, sir," said Indra, and, giving me a wink, he turned and ran back toward the road.

THIRTY-TWO

I believe Mr. Joshi, the warden, will come back as a turtle in his next life. He sat on one of the hard wooden chairs under the gazebo. Long ago, he had been appointed by the palace to protect the Borderlands' wildlife, but he almost never moved out of his office shell in Thakurdwara.

Next to him sat the forest conservator-*sahib*, then my father, creating a small half-circle. On a small table sat a pot of tea and cups, waiting to be touched. I stood some way off, to the side, so that I might hear what they were saying, without being noticed. The other drivers crouched by the fire pit chatting, waiting for some news about our fate. Only Ramji was silent, his eyes fixed on the fire.

"*Subba-sahib*, I see no progress in preparing the stable to move. As I told you, you may keep one elephant. The rest you must send away. Do you have some preparations under way that I am too blind to see?" Watermelon Belly asked.

My father stayed silent.

"I laid out the plan for this a year ago. What have you done, *Subba-sahib*? I cannot sit here all day. The Maroons have been raiding villages in the Borderlands again. I am charged with finding their hideout. It will win me a promotion when I do."

My father shot him a look that said "you are an elephant's ass," but his words came out quite differently.

"Yes, indeed, Forest Conservator-*sahib*. All the preparations are under way. But, before you go, I invite you to inspect our new elephant, a magnificent tusker."

"Yes, yes. Make it quick," said the forest conservator-*sahib*, not moving his large watermelon belly from the chair.

"After you, gentlemen," said my father, standing and letting out a piercing whistle, signaling Dilly to make sure Hira Prashad was chained to his tethering post.

Both men rose slowly and started off toward the clearing beyond the stable. They stumbled along, unused to the uneven ground. I could not believe the future of our lives depended on these two numbskulls. I followed at a distance.

When the forest conservator-*sahib* saw the large ivory on the tusker, he stopped in his tracks. "Where did you find that one, *Subba-sahib*?"

"Have you not read the proposal I sent to you, which outlines our plans to make our stable into a breeding center? You will read the strong reasons why we need to start breeding our own elephants in Nepal. Otherwise, in twenty years, perhaps less, there will be none to service the royal family."

"I read your proposal and dismissed it," he said.

The forest conservator-*sahib* continued, retaking his stance as one who would not support us. "You will never be able to breed this tusker. Look how wild he is. All that you are able to raise here are chickens and goats, and we have enough of those in the Borderlands. Stop dreaming up schemes, or I will appoint someone else to start moving your elephants out next week."

With that, Watermelon Belly left, with Mr. Joshi, the turtle, following.

My father spat on the ground as he watched the jeep at the far end of the stable grounds. The driver was having trouble turning it around, because Rona and Ritu were in the way.

He turned to me abruptly. "Today we have an important task. Come." He led me to his private grove, at the edge of the jungle. "We must pray to Ban Devi to encourage Hira Prashad to begin breeding. We must not keep her waiting."

"I think Ban Devi is angry with me. I cursed her when Devi Kali died."

But my father was already in his *jhankri* state. He closed his eyes and began chanting. I lit incense, while he chanted and swayed. He stayed like that for a long time. I prayed with him for our tusker to breed. And then, in my heart and mind, I offered an apology to Ban Devi and asked my Devi Kali to help us save the stable.

———

The rain of dried silk cotton leaves announced the arrival of winter. The days were shorter, the temperature had dropped, and we woke to a heavy mist every morning. But even so, our routine did not change. It was time to take the elephants down to the Belgadi for their daily bath. Dilly was on Man Kali, I was on Hira Prashad, and Ram Raj drove Prem Kali. Streams of water ran down the tusker's forehead. Then I noticed another stream trickled from his temple. I touched the liquid with my finger and Hira Prashad let out a low rumble. My tusker was in *musth*, ready to breed with a female.

The timing was perfect, but no one wanted to listen to us. There had been no response to our elephant-breeding center proposal from Kathmandu. It was possible that Watermelon Belly had made sure there would never be a response. Although my father never said it, the drivers sensed that our stable was nearing its end. The fear went unspoken, as did our deep sadness that any day now, the forest conservator-*sahib* would return to oversee the start of our elephant march to Chitwan.

I decided on my own to take Hira Prashad to cut a load of *babiyo* to make new ropes for the saddles. I turned my tusker past

Clear Lake and headed up toward the base of the hills, the place where my father found me years ago.

"This is where *Subba-sahib* and our mother found me, Hira Prashad," I said. His ears widened as I spoke to him.

I saw a good spot several hundred feet up the hill. I left the elephant to graze and headed up to the dense *babiyo* grass just below where giant boulders were interspersed with gnarled trees.

I started cutting, forcefully swinging my blade in anger, but soon I grew exhausted. When I straightened, something caught my eye. It was a *dhole* staring straight at me. It moved a few feet up the hill and turned his head back again. *Was he signaling me to follow him?* It was the same one, the one with the long black tail, who had crossed my path before.

I walked through the grass and when I slid down the side of a boulder near the top of the hill, I saw the rest of the pack. They were focused on something higher up, so much so that they did not notice me. They stood on alert, waiting for something. But what was it? Two more *dhole* trotted out from behind another boulder, carrying something in their jaws. They dropped it and started ripping it apart. The *dhole* who led me up the hill yipped to the others.

I stood up on a boulder to get a better look and they all stopped. The ground around them glinted in the sun. Then the *dhole* with the black tail whistled to the others and the pack vanished up the ridge.

I scrambled up to where the *dhole* had been gathered. Spilled there were a few gold coins. Higher up the hill, I saw a small opening to a cave, hidden among the brush and rocks.

I was scared to go inside, but I reasoned it was too quiet for someone to be there. The *dhole* would have sniffed him out. Still, I tiptoed into the pitch-black, so dark I could not see my hand in front of my face. I scooted back out and grabbed some *dubdube* branches to make into a torch.

The *whoosh* of horseshoe bats whispered in my ears, dodging the flame of my torch as they flew deeper into the cave. I kept shining the torch right and left, on the lookout for cobras. From the narrow entrance the space opened up into small side caves off the main hollow. I could easily stand. All at once, I stopped. I could not believe my eyes. On one side of the cave, the walls were stacked with bricks of rupees, bags of jewelry, and sacks of gold coins.

The Maroons.

THIRTY-THREE

Heavy clouds had settled on the stable by the time I had returned. A cold winter rain made everyone run for cover, except the elephants. They loved the feel of rain. I dismounted Hira Prashad and shouted for my father, who I found in the canteen talking to Rita, Dilly, and Tulsi. "I found the gold, the jewels! The Maroons have hidden it in a cave. We can catch them—"

"Calm down, Nandu. Tell us what happened."

I told them about going to cut grass and finding the *dhole*, my *dhole*.

"Let us think first. Did you leave any footprints near the cave?" my father asked.

"I did leave them," I said, and my stomach sank with fear. "I am sorry, *Subba-sahib*. I thought it was too dangerous to wait around."

"You did the right thing, Nandu. But now we must act fast. Dilly, go to the warden's bungalow. Tell him the story and ask that he alert the authorities and have them join us at the Clear Lake. You will have to stay at the bungalow to lead the way."

"Yes, sir," said Dilly, who yelled over his shoulder, for he was already off running.

Indra had returned and the other drivers were joining him to tether the elephants. "Indra, run to Thakurdwara and tell the *Budghar* we need his tractor and wagon, and tell them to alert the villagers from Mohanpur. Nandu, do you think the *Budghar's* wagon can hold all of the loot?"

I shook my head no.

"Maybe we will need Father-*sahib*'s Land Rover, too. Go run and ask him," my father said. "Tell him to meet us here in ten minutes so we can drive ahead of the tractor and prepare."

———

When the tractor was close enough, my father and Father Autry stepped out into the dirt track, gesturing for the driver to slow down. Behind the wheel was Indra. Next to him, seated on the wheel cover was Hala Ram, and there was someone on the other side. Behind them crouched a wagon full of men. I stood in the shadows, holding my father's hunting rifle for him.

"Greetings, *Subba-sahib*. I brought ten men with me, and ten more of our fast runners will be here soon," said Garibuwa.

"And I brought ten men," said the *Budghar*. "Pull the tractor next to the Land Rover, Indra, and cover it with more tree branches. We do not want the Maroons to know we are here."

My father and I realized at the same instant that the rider on the other wheel cover was Rita.

"Rita, what are you doing here? This is far too dangerous for you. Indra, why did you allow her to come?"

Indra kept his head down and so did Rita. I felt I had better speak up.

"*Subba-sahib*, we will need lookouts up in the trees, to watch for the Maroons. Rita can climb faster than any of us, and she is not afraid to go right to the top."

Rita did not look up, but I could sense she was smiling.

"Very well, then, but you stay close to Father Autry until it is time to take your lookout positions. Nandu, show me the base of the cave. We must be ready. They might be lying in wait."

A chill went up my spine. It had not occurred to me that *they* might be waiting for *us*.

"I will come with you, too, *Subba-sahib*," said Hala Ram.

"If you hear me shout, Garibuwa and *Budghar-sahib*, come running with all your men up the hill," my father said.

I felt better with another one in our group. We climbed the hill slowly, without torches. I had to lead because I knew the way, my father and Hala Ram following behind. It was treacherous going in the darkness; there was only a sliver of moonlight.

Suddenly, I saw something shiny. Perhaps it was a blessing I had not cleaned up the bags scattered by the *dhole*. Without that clue, I doubt I could have found the very same spot on the hill in the dark.

We crept toward the cave, my heart pounding. It was so quiet, but it was helping me believe that we had come back in time—before the Maroons.

There it was! I pointed out the entrance to the cave to my father. He nodded and gestured with his hand to head back down the hill.

Father Autry quietly jogged over to us. "What did you find?" he whispered. I could see Rita and Indra, hanging back.

"We searched the area, Father-*sahib*. No campfires, no sign of horses, no robbers. I believe we have arrived in time," my father said.

"Excellent."

Still, I felt better having brought the two slingshots I had left. I handed one to Hala Ram, the same one I had given him back on the Gularia Road just before the Maroons arrived.

"Thank you, Nandu," said Hala Ram. "I have waited a long time for this moment."

"Hurry. Get everything in the wagon and the Land Rover," instructed my father.

Dawn approached and the jungle was waking up. Soon a chorus of birds was singing all around us. Rita and Harka climbed up to their lookout posts to warn us of the Maroons' approach. The rest of us kept at it, ferrying bags down the hillside.

An hour later the bird chorus died down, and the jungle settled into a quiet peace. Maybe the Maroons would not return today. Maybe they would not return for a week. At least the police should be here soon, and they could set a trap.

The last bags of rupees were loaded into the Land Rover and we were ready to leave.

"We will wait here for the men who tried to kill my son," said the *Budghar*. "You may take my tractor if you wish, but I am staying here."

"The men from Mohanpur will stay, too, with our brothers from Thakurdwara," said Garibuwa. "We will live on rats and scorpions while we wait for the Maroons to return."

My father said, "Brothers, leave this to the police. We already have our revenge on them. All they have stolen from the people of the Borderlands will be returned to their owners. They have lost everything and soon they will lose their freedom."

And so it was. The Maroons were soon captured by the police, who hid at the cave and waited for the bandits to return. All except for their leader, Kalomutu, who fled into the jungle on his white stallion. His escape cost the sergeant his position and Watermelon Belly his post.

Justice.

THIRTY-FOUR

I do not know how many words a person speaks, or reads, or even thinks in a lifetime. Maybe if you string all those words together, the total is in the billions. But I do know that sometimes our fate comes down to a few sentences spoken out loud or scribbled in a letter handed to us.

"Open the letter, *Subba-sahib*, it is addressed to you," the king's emissary said.

"I will let Nandu open it, Your Grace. My eyes are troubling me these days. Nandu, read it aloud," my father commanded.

"Yes, *Subba-sahib*." My hands were trembling when I took the envelope stamped with the royal seal. I could feel the eyes of seventy-five men tracking me, watching my face for any sign.

I stared at the fine Devanagari script.

To the Senior Officer-in-Charge

of the Royal Elephant Stable,

Thakurdwara, the Borderlands:

By my direct order, this facility will be renamed the Royal
Elephant Breeding Center, and remain in Thakurdwara.
We wish you all success in your efforts.

—His Majesty Birendra Bir Bikram Shah Dev

I handed the letter back to the king's emissary to make sure I
had seen the words correctly. He smiled.

At last, I read it aloud. I looked at my father's face. For the
first time I could recall, he had tears streaming down his cheeks.

I accompanied my father that afternoon to the small clearing so he could give thanks. There, amidst the oil lamps and
candles and figurines, he paid homage to Ban Devi for looking
after us.

It struck me then—Father Autry and his peregrine falcon,
the Baba and his secret shame, and now my father selling an
elephant calf that belonged to the king—all these men had done
something that they deeply regretted. When I thought of my life
so far, I had done things I regretted, too.

It seems easy to say, "This is my fate, I cannot change it." But
we do not have to accept our lives as they are. To put these mis-
takes behind them and continue on their own paths, to make

things right with the universe, that is why I admired them so.

I bowed and thanked Ban Devi to have been found by my father, and for the Baba, and for Father Autry, and for saving our stable.

———

At daybreak, I took Hira Prashad out to cut wild sugar cane. I dropped off the grass for Indra to handle, and led my tusker to the Baba's temple. Today, to prepare for the small ceremony for our new breeding center, the Baba had mixed together dyes and food coloring. It was not to cover himself on this occasion, as *sadhus* sometimes do, but to decorate Hira Prashad.

I assisted the Baba as he painted Hira Prashad's huge head and chest. He made lines and dots of vermillion, saffron, blue sapphire, emerald green, indigo, silver, white, and tangerine. At the center of the tusker's forehead, he drew a diamond in charcoal and white powder. The Baba had no doubt seen Hira Prashad's *muti*, too.

When we returned, a gathering of officials was seated in chairs under the gazebo. Everyone from Thakurdwara was there, but some had come from far across the Borderlands. To the left of the gazebo, I could see a row of village headmen holding ceremonial gifts from their people, who were grateful to have had their possessions returned.

I climbed down from Hira Prashad, and Father Autry was there, smiling, ready to present me with a gift. Inside a wrapped package I found an embroidered tapestry of saffron and red he had specially made by a tailor in Kathmandu.

"I wanted it to be a surprise, Nandu," he said.

"Thank you, Father-*sahib*," I said, feeling that the beautiful tapestry was the perfect robe to honor Hira Prashad in our celebration.

When it was time, we moved to the front of the stable grounds, for the placing of a new sign that Father Autry had requested Ballam Abdullah's father and his sons make. It read in Devanagari and English:

ROYAL ELEPHANT BREEDING CENTER

THAKURDWARA

THE BORDERLANDS

KINGDOM OF NEPAL

My father spoke to the crowd. "Today marks the beginning of the first elephant breeding center in the Kingdom of Nepal. Thank you all for helping us to make this dream come true."

The elephants rumbled and swung their colorful trunks, and I caught sight of the Baba standing near Hira Prashad, his hand resting against the elephant's belly. One by one, the village headmen offered their gifts to my father, who took his time and bowed graciously to each one, truly grateful. Then there were a few boring speeches from the officials from Nepalganj, after which the crowd happily dispersed to go enjoy the feast.

In the crowd, I spotted Ballam, who had come back from Future Scholars just for the celebration.

"I am so glad you are here!" I said.

"Yes, Nandu, me too."

I led my friend across the grounds to where people were assembling for an official photo. Hira Prashad was in the middle, wearing his bright tapestry.

"Now, Nandu, it is time for our photo. I want to remember this day," my father said.

So did I.

My father summoned Rita so that we would be in the center of the picture. He whispered to us, "Without you two, the elephants would be on their way to Chitwan."

When I took my place at his side, he threw his arm around me and held me close. It is my favorite memory—my family, my whole family, in one place, smiling and happy. For so long, ever since my father and Devi Kali found me in a strange land, far from where my people lived, I wondered how I got here, how I would ever fit in. Would I always be the odd one with the rich brown skin? Now I could stop wondering. This is my home, here with my father and the elephants. This has always been my home. At last it was perfectly clear.

The main group broke up to join the feast, but other photos were being taken. Father Autry and I stood side by side for one, but the Baba refused to be photographed. I remembered his story to me and understood. Then I had a better idea for creating another memory of the day.

"Father-*sahib*, may I take you and the Baba for a ride on Hira Prashad?"

"Oh, I would be most honored," he said. The Baba nodded enthusiastically.

"May I come, too?" Suddenly, Rita was there, eager to join in.

"Next time, it will be your turn," I said.

I rode into the forest just beyond camp, where we saw a pair of Asian paradise flycatchers fly fast and free, directly across our path, their long white tail feathers floating on the breeze.

I pointed and Father Autry put his hand on my shoulder. We had no need to speak any words.

When we returned from our short tour, I commanded Hira Prashad to kneel so that Father Autry and the Baba could step down his back leg to more easily reach the ground. Before I could even say a word, Rita was climbing up, taking her place behind me on the saddle. We rode into the jungle, where we saw a flock of jungle babblers gather on a branch, but both they and we were silent as we floated by them. I turned back to look at her. Rita was looking up, of course, into the tree canopy, not wanting to miss a thing.

Hira Prashad moved powerfully and silently along the trail. His graceful gait lulled me deep into thought. In that moment, the past year came flooding back to me: the threat of the stable closing; the attack on Mohanpur; the death of the Maroon; my nights in jail. I felt the remorse all over again thinking of the paradise flycatchers. Then the death of my Devi Kali, which dropped me to the bottom of my life; and finding Hira Prashad, which pulled me back up. Finally, I thought of the *dhole*, and all they had done.

What might happen in the coming year, I wondered. What if the breeding center fails? What if my father dies and leaves us?

Hira Prashad's rumbling broke me from my trance. I was riding my elephant through my beloved jungle. There was no better place for me to be than right here. What did the Baba once tell me? "My dear friend," he had said, "there is nothing to be gained by dwelling on what is past, or worrying about what may or may not come to pass. All we have is this moment right in front of us. It is precious, and the more you stay present, the more peace you will feel in your heart."

"Where are you, Nandu?" asked Rita, poking me in the ribs. "You are so quiet."

"I am right here."

Hira Prashad scared up a black partridge, and it shot like a missile across our path.

"Rita, I am so glad you came up with the idea for saving our stable." I said. "Thank you." She did not reply, so I shifted to see her face.

Now she was the one in a trance, looking past the edge of the forest to the waving elephant grass beyond.

"So, Rita, how do you feel up here on the great Hira Prashad?" I asked her in accented English, doing my best imitation of Father Autry.

She dropped her chin and looked straight into my eyes.

"Invincible."

IMPORTANT TERMS

Borderlands, the—the low flat land (elevation around six hundred feet) along the border between Nepal and India at the base of the Himalayas; where this story takes place

budghar—the headman in a Tharu village

caste system—in Nepal, people are divided into castes or ranks with the Hindu Brahmins as highest caste and Tharus and Tamangs of low-caste or status; elephant drivers are almost always of low-caste; level of education also often follows caste

chapatti—flat bread, often eaten in place of rice

dal—stewed lentils, served over rice

Dashain—a fifteen-day national holiday in Nepal, celebrated at the end of the summer monsoon

dhole—another name for the Asiatic wild dog; a wild canid that hunts in packs and is common in the Borderlands

driver—each elephant in the stable has three drivers:

> **phanit**—the head driver
>
> **pachuwa**—the second-in-command of the elephant
>
> **mahout**—the entry-level driver

jalebis—a treat made from wheat flour, shaped into coils, deep fried, and soaked in syrup

jhankri—a spirit man

Kali—the last name of every female elephant; Kali refers to a powerful Hindu goddess

khukri—the traditional curved knife used by Nepalese men and made famous by the British Gurkha soldiers

kuchi—the Nepali word for elephant treats consisting of unhusked rice, rock salt, and crude sugar wrapped in leaves

maharajah—king or ruler

musth—a state of heightened aggression and activity experienced by adult male elephants ready to breed

muti—a precious gem rumored to be present in the foreheads of brave elephants

namaste—the traditional greeting among Nepalese, meaning literally "I bow to the God in you"

nilgai—the largest antelope of Asia; also called the blue bull

Prashad or Gajh—the last name of male elephants

raksi—the home-distilled rice wine of the Borderlands

rupee—the name of the currency in Nepal

sadhu—the Nepali name for a Hindu holy man

sahib—similar to "sir," the word that Nepalese and Indians attach to titles or names to show respect (for example, one might refer to a teacher as teacher-*sahib*)

samosa—a triangular, deep-fried turnover filled with vegetables or meat and spices shaman—a person with special powers who can engage spirits, use magic, and foretell the future

shambo—term of respect used to address an older Tamang

Subba-sahib—title given to the officer in charge of an elephant stable

Tharu—the indigenous people of the Borderlands

thulo manche—Nepalese slang for a big shot

Tihar—the five-day Hindu festival of light, typically falling after the rice harvest

tusker—a bull elephant that sports huge ivory

Common Elephant Commands Used by Drivers

agat—forward

beit—kneel down

chhi—let alone; drop

hikh—attack; close in sideways

khol beit—drag hind legs to allow a driver to shinny up them to the saddle

meil—get up

pasar—kneel over to one side

raa—stand squarely and stop what you are doing

sarbeit—sit up straight on all fours

AUTHOR'S NOTE

One measure of a happy life is to know a second childhood, especially when the first one seemed lacking in adventure. Mine took place in the most spectacular setting imaginable: an unspoiled Nepalese jungle at the base of the Himalayas, home to tigers and pythons and peacocks.

I first arrived in Nepal in 1975, and soon moved to Bardia district (the Borderlands) at a time when this remote kingdom, closed to the outside for centuries, cracked open again. I lived here for nearly two and a half years, estimating the local tiger population. I spent over a hundred nights in the jungle—not just to count and photograph the elusive tiger, but to dare myself to stay out alone in one of the wildest spots in Asia.

On one of those nights, while staring at the star-filled sky, the idea for this novel took root.

I returned to Nepal eleven years later, this time for five years, working for the Smithsonian Institution. I led a field team that studied rhinos and tigers; we often rode elephants through the twenty-five-foot-tall grass. I lived between the government elephant stable and a separate elephant breeding center, each about half a mile away, and only a few yards upwind from our own private stable of five females used for research. I can still smell the burning elephant dung.

I have returned to Nepal many times since, and nearly thirty years later, Nanda Singh's story has finally come to be. I thank the Nepalese friends I have made over the years. They are the most brave and gentle people I have ever met. Their companionship stays with me forever.

Eric Dinerstein

ACKNOWLEDGMENTS

Nanda Singh had *Subba-sahib* as his jungle tutor. I had Gagan Singh, a game scout employed by the Royal Karnali-Bardia Wildlife Reserve. Gagan showed me how to track tigers on foot and taught me the local names of everything in the jungle. The Tharus of Thakurdwara were gracious hosts and served me too much rice beer and hot chilis. In Chitwan, five years of research on the Smithsonian Tiger Ecology Project in the company of our outstanding trackers—Vishnu Lama, Harka Man Lama, Bul Bahadur Lama, Man Bahadur Lama, Ram Kumar Aryal, Man Singh, and Keshav Giri—filled in the rest of my jungle education. Our five elephants, Chanchal Kali, Prem Kali, Mel Kali, Kirti Kali, and Man Kali inspired me to write this book. Ram Lotan and Baddhai Lal Tharu, the officers-in-charge of the government elephant stable and the Smithsonian stable, respectively, served as my role models for the character of *Subba-sahib*. Gyan Bahadur Tharu, Bir Bahadur Lama, Phirta Tharu, Brij Lal Tharu, Pashupat Tharu, Badri Tharu, Ram Raj Tharu, Arjun Kumal, Maila Kumal, Ram Bahadur Gurung, and Ram Ji Tharu taught me to trust and honor elephants.

Hemanta and Sushma Mishra taught me so much about Nepal and, along with Chris Wemmer and the Smithsonian, made my stay possible. The Nepal government gave me permission to live and work in Chitwan. Annie Bruno and Jonathan Cobb read several drafts and helped shape this book. Nancy Sherman, Lori Price, Mimi Rekstad, Britta Justesen, Marshall and Jamee Field, John Lehmkuhl, Donna Kutchma, Maris Miles, Trudy Nicholson, Minette Glazer, Paige Grant, Ken May, Tunan Pan, Allie Stadler, and Holly Dinerstein were also early readers, and Trishna Gurung, Anup Joshi, and Shubash Lohani ensured fealty to Nepalese custom and culture. My mother, Eleanor, and Paula Wolff listened to me read them an early draft. Generous grants from Roger and Vicki Sant and Jeffrey Berenson allowed me to keep my day job and write at night, and Steve D'Esposito and the wonderful colleagues at Resolve, Inc. gave me a home to continue my conservation work. My agent, Richard Abate, assisted by Melissa Kahn, saw something salvageable in an early manuscript and stuck with me. His great insights enriched this story and also found me the best editor one could hope for in Tracey Keevan at Disney Hyperion. Her gentle persuasion, constant encouragement, and sublime editing skills made our collaboration a joy for me to experience. Finally, I would like to thank my close reader and wife, Ute, who heard me utter more times than I care to mention, "I'm almost done."

BELGADI RIVER

GREAT SAND BAR RIVER

MOHANPUR

GOBRELA

Royal
Hunting
Grounds

Father
Autry's
Bungalow

Baba's Temple

THAKURDWARA

Elephant
Stable

Northern Ridge

CLEAR LAKE

Dhole's Cave

NEPAL

THE BORDERLANDS

INDIA

CENTRAL BORDERLANDS

BABAI RIVER

CENTRAL
BORDERLANDS JUNGLE